# Changing Tides

a novel by

Jessica Biron

Edit et Cetera Ltd.
www.familybookhouse.com
Member: Colorado Independent Publishers Asso.

© 2006 by Jessica Biron

This novel is a work of fiction. No similarity to individuals living or dead is intended, and any such resemblance that may occur is coincidental.

Author's Cover Photo: Rheault Photography, Manchester, New Hampshire

Cover Design: Linda Lane

ISBN: 0-9769989-1-2

## Dedication

To my mother, Linda, without whom this would never have been published, and my father, David, who always asked "when," and never "if," I would write a book.

# Chapter One

"I hope you'll like it here."

The words flowed out of her mouth, but the woman's eyes said something different.

"I'm sure I will."

Yeah, right. I would love it here with these parents I didn't love, this sister who looked at me with hate, this brother with his wide, innocent eyes. I would love it here with these people who took away my mother and threw her in jail. I would just pretend to be alive and still breathing.

Home sweet home was Whispering Pines, a summer cottage in Maine. It wasn't really a cottage, but a house. John told me it's a five-minute bike ride from the beach. John claimed to be my father. I didn't have a father, just Mother. And Mother and I lived in an apartment half the size of this so-called home where I didn't belong.

Whispering Pines loomed two stories high, its sides covered with cedar shake shingles. The roof sloped down at odd angles to the top of the porch, framing a single lonely window that looked out on the street. The front porch wasn't screened in. Paint peeled off in thick chunks from the railing. A wooden swing hung in a corner, and four Adirondack chairs sat on it. For *four* family members.

I followed John upstairs to one of the bedrooms. Even though scrutinizing the house was better than thinking about the people, I didn't bother to take in any more details of the place. I hated it because it wasn't home.

John set my suitcases down on the floor. "This used to be Mimi's room. We thought you might need some privacy, so she's in Ricky's room now. You get the room all to yourself."

He looked at me. I stared back, hoping the coldness of my glare conveyed my lack of concern for such trivial facts. It must have worked. He shoved his hands into his pockets and spoke to the floor.

"Dinner will be ready in an hour."

He left, pulling the door closed behind him. I wished he would slam it.

It was a small, square room. A twin bed was tucked into a corner, covered with a worn yellow comforter. A small wooden desk sat in front of the only window. The window was round, like a porthole on a ship. Every time I looked at it, I thought about screaming, "Land Ahoy!" The chair was painted the same buttery shade as the comforter. A dresser that didn't match the bed was against the other wall. One of the drawers stuck out about four inches and wouldn't close when I pushed on it.

The white walls had little thumbtack holes sprinkled across them like freckles. Mimi must have taken all her stuff out when she moved in with Ricky. I didn't bother to unpack because I was leaving just as soon as they realized it was all a mistake. Instead, I sat on the bed, feeling it sag under my weight, and listened to Mimi downstairs. John must have left because she didn't say a word when he was around.

"I don't want her in my room, Mom. It's *my* room. I want it back!"

"Now Miami..."

"Don't call me Miami! I hate that name. It's Mimi. That girl isn't ours. She *isn't* my sister. She doesn't belong with us. I hate her. I hated her the minute I saw her."

"Of course she's your sister. You look so much alike," Anna said. She sounded tired. "Don't talk that way, Mimi, darling. She just needs to settle in, to become part of the family.

"She'll never be a part of the family, never! And she's not my sister. I wish she was dead!"

The last line was accompanied by her stomping footsteps on the stairs. Without knocking, she swung the bedroom door open, banging it into the wall and leaving a dent where the doorknob hit.

"I hope you're happy here! You ruined this family once. Don't think you can do it again!"

Her anger hung on every word, a hot volcano spewing her vile contempt for my presence.

I stiffened. "Don't worry about it. I'll be leaving soon. I wouldn't want to be a part of this family anyway."

My voice sounded reptilian, sinister. I felt like a mob boss telling some guy that I was about to shoot him. So calm and cool, like it was just another part of his job. Meaningless.

She had no comeback. She just stood there, her hands clawing at the doorframe. Then she whipped around, running down the hall into what I assumed was Ricky's room. I heard her scream at him.

"Get out! Get out!"

Poor kid. I shut the door, the click almost inaudible.

Picking up my backpack, I pulled out my journal and put it on the dresser. I kept a journal, not a diary. Mother gave me a diary when I was in second grade. I wrote in it until I was in fifth. On the day I was told to pack my things, I read every page of nonsense in it. Stupid hopes and dreams. Stories about boys I liked and the chance encounters I had with them. How much I wanted a cat, a little white one I'd name Fluffy. Mother wouldn't get me one because pets weren't allowed in our apartment building.

I stopped writing after fifth grade.

It wasn't until eighth grade that I began to record my thoughts, this time in a plain leather-bound journal. No

Disney characters or flowers on the cover. And I didn't write all the stupid nothings of my life anymore. I started recording my deep thoughts, ones on life and death, love and hate. I wrote poetry. I used to draw sketches in it, but they weren't any good, so I stopped.

It was funny, the poetry I wrote. Not proper poetry, it didn't always rhyme. It didn't have hidden meanings that the average person couldn't comprehend. No Shakespearean sonnets or Wordsworth's great poems. I just wrote to express myself. To express what I wanted to say, what I could say, but never what I would say.

The pages slipped through my fingers. Countless words flew by, countless moments. My finger stopped and I read.

*What is a rose without the sun?*
*What is beauty without happiness?*
*The rose is red, it graces the earth,*
*But without the sun,*
*It withers and dies.*

I remembered the day I'd written that. It was in May, after school, the kind of day when the wind blew just right and kept you cool, but not too cold. I sat at the desk in my room, thinking about that girl at school. Every school has one—little miss popular, sunshine, blue-eyes, heaven itself on earth. But she was so sad. She always smiled and was cheerful, laughing with her friends. I was in five of her classes and saw her everyday. She was never in a bad mood, never had an unpleasant thing to say about anyone. That's how I knew she was sad; she was always happy. Perpetual happiness is a mask worn by an actress struggling to go on.

I sat there, thinking about her. I'd always despised her flawless complexion and endless supply of boyfriends. When I wrote the poem, I focused on her awful future. She had everything. No one could have everything. One day she would look around and see nothing. I felt a deep sense of satisfaction at the thought of her desolate, alone. The not-so-perfect people in the world tell themselves this—that perfect people would one day fall, and it would be a long fall.

The next day as I headed to biology class, I saw her walking with books in her arms, leaning forward as if walking into the wind. And I felt so sorry for her. Sorry for her beautiful, sorrowful life.

Roses wither and die.

## Chapter Two

John spent his weekdays in Manchester. I had to ask where that was. Mimi almost choked on her milk at dinner.

"It's in New Hampshire, stupid," she said. "Where we live."

That dinner qualified as the worst in my life. Stiff. Tense. I could barely inhale enough of the heavy air down to keep breathing. John sat at the head of the table, Anna, his wife, at the foot. Mimi and Ricky sat across from me, their adversary. Ricky ate non-stop, staring at his plate. He had two helpings of peas. I'd never met a nine year old who liked peas. He wouldn't meet my eyes. Mimi did, her angry stare penetrating right through me. She was bursting at the seams to say something mean. I knew that was why she jumped at my ignorance.

As soon as she spoke, John told her to hush up. I loved being in religious households, where the words "shut up" were considered harsh. He explained that during the rest of the year they lived in Manchester. He talked to me like I was an idiot, with slow patience, enunciating every word. He told me that he was a doctor, a pediatrician.

"I have to be down there during the week," he said, "and a lot of the weekends too. But I'll come up when I can."

It was Sunday, time for him to leave. He kissed Anna on the cheek, hugged Ricky, and yelled at Mimi. He stood in front of me, holding his right hand out in an awkward gesture. Light brown hair feathered his fingers and peeked out from his jacket at his wrist. I shook his warm, dry hand. He told me to call if anything was wrong or something. I took his proffered business card, feeling like a client.

"Just ask for Dr. Burton," he said, "and they'll get me for you."

Anna walked with him onto the porch. His low voice sounded like gravel and harmonized with the crickets chirping under the porch.

"Don't lose her like you did last time, okay?" He spoke in the same idiot voice he'd used with me.

She mumbled something back.

"I'm counting on you, Anna. Don't be a complete failure as a mother."

Then the engine in his white Bentley started up, and he backed out of the dirt driveway. Anna stood there for a good five minutes, long after he was out of sight.

Mother would have slapped him right across the face for treating her like that. She would have told him what a jerk he was and to never talk to her like that again. Anna just stood there, slumped over. She hadn't said a word in protest.

## Chapter Three

A week passed, and I learned to detest the beach. The sand drove me crazy. It stuck to my legs, hurting when I rubbed in sunscreen. The incessant pounding of the waves drove me to distraction. And the people...

The people were something else, loud and annoying. Little kids ran around in polka dot bathing suits, kicking sand on everyone. Old men sauntered by in Speedos. Women wore itty bitty bikinis that did not belong on forty-year-old mothers. The teenagers made me sick, walking by on the damp low-tide sand. They held hands and, in love for the glorious summer months, seemed oblivious to everything else. Yesterday I'd tripped over a couple snuggled in the sand. I apologized over and over, but they didn't even notice.

Mimi was in her element. At thirteen, she had just discovered the effects of a skimpy bathing suit on thirteen-year-old boys. She liked to walk by a group of them, swinging her hips from side to side, convinced she was the best thing since Elvis Presley shocked innocent America. When she talked to boys, she giggled like she was stuck in flirtation mode. I thought she sounded ditzy. When she was with her best friend, Lana, she sounded much more sophisticated. They talked about world issues such as clothes and shades of nail polish. Their favorite activity was watching an older boy body surf in the waves. His name was Jimmy or Johnny or something like that. The two of them could have been Siamese twins. They whispered with their heads close together whenever I was around. Lana learned to hate me just as much as Mimi.

I knew Anna hated me too. She was nice all the time, never raising her voice. Ricky broke the kitchen window with a rock, and she wasn't even angry. She just used duct tape to fasten a plastic bag over it and called up the company to order a new one. There wasn't a big rush to get it fixed because John wasn't coming up for the weekend. He called, saying he was too busy.

I didn't realize she detested me when I first met her. I had to watch for signs because she never voiced her true feelings. It was the way she looked at me and her tone of voice, just a little different from the way she spoke to Mimi and Ricky. Maybe she felt that way because I was the reason that John was angry with her. He blamed the kidnapping on her. Somebody said it happened in a grocery store, a Shop 'N' Save. We were in the cereal aisle, and she'd turned her back on me. When she turned around, Cheerios in hand, I was gone. At least that's the story they told the judge.

As much as I hated to admit it, I did look like that family. It must have been a strange coincidence, a twist of fate. Mother was my family. Those people were just pretenders. Actors in snazzy costumes. They didn't want me, not even Ricky. John liked the idea of me, his perfect first-born child. If I had found another girl whose name was Mary to take my place, he wouldn't have noticed. Fake-Mary would have worked just as well.

The sun pounded down on my face. I could feel it turning red. Mimi and her cohort stood down by the water, waves lapping at their feet. It was high tide, when the ocean climbs up to the slope of the beach. If you went out into the water three feet, you would drop a good foot down without warning, and the undertow would pull you further out. But during low tide, the ocean receded back about twenty-six yards, revealing wet smooth sand. The hot yellow sand of the beach sloped down to it. Separating the yellow and the brown sands were tide pools at the base of the slope, wide puddles of salt-water connected by ribs of sand. Kids loved playing in these, digging with their shovels to put up moats and walls. The deeper and wider the pool, the more they seemed to enjoy it.

Ricky had a set of plastic animals he played with. They were so realistic, right down to the protruding fangs painted on the tiger. He played and played with those things for hours on end. Although he was a sweet kid, he was a loner. Like me.

Yesterday during low tide I'd gone down to his pool. He was making intricate castles out of wet sand on his walls. He would pick up a handful, then let it dribble through his fingers.

"Do you know how to make a drizzle castle?" he asked, intent on his task.

"No."

"It's easy. Just pick up some wet sand, and let it drizzle down."

I picked up a handful, then released it as he demonstrated. Chunks fell out, forming the base. Near the end a thin, almost continuous drizzle came out of my clenched fists. It formed delicate spires on a fascinating little castle. The drips layered on each other, creating something both fragile and beautiful in its simplicity.

He gestured to the journal in my other hand.

"You write in that a lot. What's in it?"

"My thoughts, my poems. I write about…a lot of things."

For some strange reason I felt an urge to share with this little boy. To communicate a private thought, something I've never shown anyone before. To unlock the dark room and let in some light.

"Would you like to hear one of my poems?"

He looked up with an eager expression. "Yes!"

I browsed through the pages, unsure of what to read to a nine-year-old boy. He smiled up at me, and I wondered whether it was such a good idea.

"Here's one. I wrote it about poetry. It's not that good or anything."

"That's okay."

I began to read.

*A poem*
*What is that*
*Soft sweet music*
*That never sounds flat*
*Must it rhyme, why no*
*A poem sings*
*However it goes*
*And must the words*
*Be loud and angry*
*Or soft as butterfly kisses*
*Or deep as the rain*
*A poem*
*Is a rare and priceless gem*
*Treasure it*

Ricky sat in silence. I concentrated on the sand sticking to his shoulder, the soft flakes against the already tan background. I shouldn't have read that, shouldn't have shared, should have kept it to myself like I always did...

"I liked it."

And he smiled again, going back to play with his animals. The breeze played with his hair, fluffing it up. Maybe not everyone in that family hated me. It was only then that I noticed the twin shadows in front of me. Twin girl shadows.

"A poem, what is that," Mimi sneered.

Lana was trying to stifle her laughter.

"That was the stupidest thing I've ever heard!"

"Oh yeah?" I said, my tone threatening.

Before I could rise out of my crouch, they ran away laughing. I watched their slim, tan bodies slip in and out of all the people. Stupid little girls.

## Chapter Four

A soft knocking on the door surprised me.

"You can come in," I said.

Anna poked her head in; then her body followed. She seemed uncomfortable as she moved into the room.

"I noticed you don't like the beach," she said.

I felt embarrassed and couldn't understand why.

"Not really."

"You don't have to come anymore. You can stay at Whispering Pines, or you can come if you want to. It's up to you."

She paused like she wanted to say something else. Her v-neck t-shirt shifted, and I could see her bra strap. I would have laughed at Mother, making fun of her. We would have joked around, teasing each other. Maybe we would have gone shopping afterwards or watched old movies on T.V. But Mother was in jail, and Anna was not the type of woman you told that her bra strap was showing.

"Okay."

She seemed relieved, like a great burden was lifted from her shoulders. She turned to leave, then paused.

"But tomorrow, tomorrow is Saturday. John will be here. You'll come to the beach with us then."

"Okay."

An hour later, I watched from out the bay front window. They rode their bikes down to the beach. Anna had a white cart attached to hers, an ingenious device chock full of beach stuff. A long, thin handle locked the cart onto the bike under the seat. The cart was made out of wooden slats painted white, forming a deep box shape. There were spaces between the slats as wide as my hand. A little triangular reflector flag attached to a black spring flapped off one side.

Once they reached the beach, they parked at the end of the street, locking their bikes up against the fence. Anna pushed the cart up the wooden walkway made out of boards lined up together, forming a flat path. It climbed up through the dune grass, protected by a waist-high, maroon colored fence with fading paint. Posted signs warned of fines incurred if you walked on the dune grass.

So I watched them bike up the street, long legs pumping, until they were out of sight. I told Anna that I would wash the dishes for her. She seemed tense all the time, worry lines tight on her face. If I were married to a man like John, I'd be tense all the time too.

The warm suds slid over the dishes, making them shine in the light. My hands were busy, but my mind traveled among my memories.

I remembered Mother. She was so beautiful, with long, blond, wavy hair and intense brown eyes, a combination not seen very often. Her teeth were a little bit crooked, but her brilliant smile made such small details unimportant. Hers was not the beauty of a goddess, but the beauty of nature in all its glory. But what I remembered most was her laugh. Not the tinkling of a brook running over stones, but the booming laugh of a warm summer day. The kind of laugh that filled you to the brim, made your cup overflow.

The sink overflowed, trickles of water escaping the raised edge. I shut off the water and pulled the plug. While drying the dishes, I decided to explore rather than sweat in the house's high humidity. I didn't want to be in that place, which reeked of raw emotions, all negative.

I escaped out the screen door, flip-flops clattering down the stairs. To the left was the road to the beach; to the right was a crossroad and then a dead end. I turned to the right and walked down to the crossroad. It attached to the main road, which was the emergency route. We had driven up it on our way to Whispering Pines. Few houses sat beside it, just overlapping pine trees, but many cars traveled up and down it every day. If I took a left, I could walk all the way to the highway. But if I took a right, I would walk through the center of Ocean Park and up a wooden walkway to the beach, provided my path was straight.

My flip-flops made a dull flapping sound as I walked to the right. Cars full of happy beach-going families drove by. Low beach chairs crowded the back windows, competing with coolers and sand shovels for space.

Five minutes down the road and across from me was the Temple. Shaped like a hexagon, it had a tall, peaking roof and white sides with green trimmings. The Temple didn't have a particular faith attached to it. I'd asked why the Burtons didn't go to church there since it was so close. That had earned me another snicker from Mimi, but no answer. Two smaller buildings flanked it, identical in their color scheme. Both were memorials to some dead guy. I wondered what it was like to be important enough to have a building erected in your honor. Since Ocean Park was so small, they were probably the builders of the first ice cream shop.

I crossed over to the cement sidewalk in front of it. What had started out as a line of indistinguishable gray squares was decaying into a rock path. A sign near the Temple advertised for a movie showing next Tuesday. *The Italian Job* was going to be playing. Action movies weren't my favorites.

I passed by many houses, each a variation of its neighbor. A tennis court sat across another street. People still played this late in the morning, their bodies glistening. The sinews in their legs strained, the chords in their arms visible. They moved in a strange dance, feet beating out a rapid cadence, swinging their rackets in time to an invisible tune.

Farther down was a cute little gift shop, accessible by a sagging screen door. I went in and looked at all the sweatshirt options with which to express my love for Ocean Park. A rack of postcards displayed all the different views of the beach. I picked up a glossy one, wondering where the peaceful and scenic beach had been when I was on it. The shop connected to a little ice cream parlor. The place had five booths and two little white café tables, as well as outside seating. It served lunch and dinner in addition to ice cream. I didn't have any money with me. If I had been living with Mother, I would have taken some out of her purse to buy myself an ice cream. She wouldn't have minded. Why should she? She was my Mother. What was mine was hers, and what was hers was mine.

If only the Burton family had left us alone. Not one of them wanted me, so why did I stay?

## Chapter Five

*I'm suffocating*
*In this narrow room,*
*Bare white walls,*
*Don't you see?*
*What you see isn't me.*
*You don't know me,*
*For that matter neither do I,*
*No one knows me.*
*So stop it with the box,*
*With the bare white walls,*
*I'm suffocating.*

John came late last night. We had chicken and potato salad for dinner. I hated onions, and I thought Anna put them in just to annoy me. I was picking out all the miniscule pieces when John announced in a casual tone that Mother was in jail.

"Serves her right," Mimi smirked. "She was nothing but a fat liar anyway."

"You take that back." My voice rose to a high-pitched cry. "Take that back *now*!"

"Why? Why take back the truth? She stole a little girl from her mother. Stole her right out of the store! Though I guess it was a good thing. Too bad she couldn't keep you."

I threw my plate at her head. It hit her on her forehead, off to the right side. She fell out of her chair onto the floor. I didn't remember anything else because I was running, running away, out the door, down the stairs, down the street. It didn't matter where, I just had to run. My lungs were burning, my legs were exhausted, and the pain felt so good. On and on I ran, on to the beach. I hated the beach. I ran up the wooden walkway that blazed a trail through the dune grass. I ran and threw myself down on the sand.

And I cried. I hadn't cried in months. A dam broke under the pressure, a well overflowed, and hot, salty tears ran down my face and dripped off my jaw.

At first they were angry tears, scalding my cheeks. Then they were tears of sadness, a soft regretful river. At last they were tears of acceptance. Tears that knew I had lost, white flag tears. I poured my soul upon the sand through my eyes.

Mother was not my mother. All my life I'd believed her to be mine, an integral part of me. All my life I had believed in her, in her solidness and immutability. Last year it was ripped away from me, and a piece of my heart was torn out. Last year I had been found, without ever knowing I had been lost. Last year was the end of the beginning, and the beginning of the end.

They did DNA tests. I refused to believe. They showed me pictures of my real family. I credited the resemblance to pure coincidence. The tear-stained letter from my real family failed to move me. But the law was rock solid. I could throw myself down over and over, but the rock would not budge.

So I went with them, and she went to jail. My other half, my better half, was nothing more than a criminal. She was a childless woman who had wanted more than anything else to be a mother, so she had stolen another woman's child. I knew it then. I could no longer pretend that the lies were true. The evidence had been laid out in front of me, and reality drove it home. But I knew that Mother had raised me with much more love than I was getting at the hands of the Burtons. And a mother is more than someone who gives birth, as Anna has proven. A mother is the one who loves you.

That was the night that I fell in love with the beach. As I lay there, alone in my cold gray life, the waves rocked against the shore. The soft slap of the sea against the sand became a gentle lullaby. It was dark, quiet, peaceful. The sea was all there was, and it was exquisite.

I walked down to it, dipping my toes in the surf. As far as I could see, it was black and calm. The sky dipped down and was one with it. I didn't feel like crying anymore, the stillness of the water instilling something into my soul.

As I walked back into the house, John rose up from his seat at the kitchen table to intercept me. Anna's face was red, not from crying, but from the handprint on her cheek. She sat unmoving, staring at the grains of the table.

"Madonna," he said. Their name for me.

"My name is Mary."

I slipped past him and climbed the stairs. He didn't follow me. My mother may have been a crooked woman with a crooked soul to go with her crooked teeth, but she named me Mary. And Mary was my name.

I sat at my desk, watching the rain spatter down. I heard them downstairs, the clattering of dishes and the riot of the T.V., but I didn't go down. John knocked, like nothing had happened, and asked if I wanted to go get some ice cream. I didn't bother replying. He hesitated outside the door for a few moments, and I heard his breath bouncing off it when he must have leaned close. Then he walked back downstairs. The car started up in the driveway and rumbled down the street. I didn't watch them drive away.

Instead I just sat there, studying the poem I had written two years ago. I was suffocating in this house with this family. Like a large puzzle piece that doesn't match in the little puzzle, I didn't fit in. Nor did I want to.

I remained there for the better part of an hour before picking up my blue pen.

*Four walls*
*All bars*
*This is my mind.*
*My own judge.*
*Jury.*
*Jailor.*
*Who can I blame*
*But me?*
*No one else imprisoned me.*
*No one else can set me free.*

## Chapter Six

I went to the beach every night. Anna didn't care. I liked to go around six o'clock after the people had gone home. The light was at a perfect angle, the sun setting a warm glow on the sands, so different from the harsh brilliance of the day. The ocean wasn't as boisterous as during the day, nor as serene as at night. It had energy that expended itself as needed. The waves tossed themselves in joy, as though celebrating the completion of another day.

The sand was still warm between my toes. If it was low tide, I walked along the damp sand revealed by the ocean, ankle deep in the waves. I walked to the river, which was to the right of where the walkway ended. To the left was the Center with the pier and its accompanying crowds. I didn't know the river's name, the gentle current that flowed down to kiss the ocean. At low tide you could walk in it, the water just skimming your toes. At high tide it was a raging beast, almost impossible to cross. It was a good place to find sea glass. A small jar in my room held my collection. There were rules to collecting sea glass. It had to be rounded and smooth with no sharp edges. Beer bottle browns were worth one point each, seafoam greens were two, and azure blues counted as three points. Any other color was worth five. I kept a mental tally as I slipped the pieces into my jean pocket. My best find was a tiny piece of baby powder pink. I imagined that it came from a perfume bottle of some kind, dropped into the ocean by a chic woman from her yacht.

An older woman who did the same thing sometimes walked side by side with me, and we combed the sand with our eyes. I didn't say a word to her, and I didn't need to. Just a slight nod and smile were enough.

Her silver hair, often gathered back into a braid, swung down her back in time to her steps. She wore loose cotton sweaters and khaki pants rolled up to the knees. She didn't appear old despite her age and dress. Her hands were a work of art. Ropy and knotted from years of labor, her fingers thin but strong. Piano hands. They were bronzed by the sun and given a life of their own.

Hers reminded me of a hand I had seen on the subway once. The lady was old and stooped. I had gotten up to offer her my seat, but she waved me back down with her cane.

"I don't need a seat. I'm not old yet," she'd said. Her hand had gripped the pole, fingers catching at each other. The knuckles were prominent in my memory. Hard and pronounced, they'd seen all the world had to offer and met it head on.

The silver lady's hands defined her too. A little worse for the wear, they were still going strong, still beautiful.

## Chapter Seven

"Excuse me. Excuse me."

"What?"

I turned around, wondering who could want me, and saw the boy from the ice cream parlor. He was holding up my wallet, the chestnut leather providing an odd contrast with his bronzed skin.

"You forgot this."

John had given me some money the last time he was up in Maine. I think he felt bad for me. I didn't see how a crisp twenty dollar bill was supposed to make me feel better about my life.

"Thanks. I should be more careful."

"Yeah, you should. I mean…"

His cheeks turned an interesting shade of flamingo pink. He was quite handsome.

"It's okay, I know what you meant."

"Jimmy. Jimmy Boswell."

He held his hand out. It had calluses from scooping so much ice cream from the large white cartons.

"Mary." I pause. "Mary Burton."

"Nice to meet you, Mary."

"Likewise, Jimmy."

We smiled at each other. It was the kind of smile when you both smile at once, and then the smile keeps on going, fueled by each other's grins. And then because I could not be in the vicinity of a cute boy for more than five minutes without doing something stupid, I dropped my ice cream cone. On his foot. We both stared at it for a second, then cracked up with laughter, the grins stretching wide enough to break. Why a chocolate ice cream cone on a foot was so funny, I had no idea. But we couldn't stop laughing. My sides hurt, and I hugged them to keep from bursting.

"Come on. I'll buy you a new one."

"Oh, no, it was my fault. Don't worry. I'm so sorry I'm such a klutz." I was babbling.

He smiled at me again, and I just about melted down with my ice cream. It was like an artificial sun, guaranteed to warm up the coldest day. We walked back together, the ice cream melting and sticking to his foot. He didn't seem to care. He walked behind the counter, measuring three scoops into a waffle cone. Then he put the cone in a bowl, and handed it to me with a spoon.

"Just in case," he said.

I went for my wallet, but he waved me off with the dripping ice cream scoop.

"It's on the house,"

"Are you allowed to do that?"

"Not really." He sent me a wide and cheeky grin. It was infectious, and I found myself grinning back. What was it with this guy and his smiles?

"Listen," he said. "I get out of work in an hour. Maybe I could meet you somewhere, and we could go to the beach or something."

"Sure. It's my favorite time to go there."

We walked hand in hand on the beach, Jimmy and I. I'd just met him and already felt as if I'd known him forever. When he talked to me, I felt like I was in eternal sunshine. My heart filled up, and my soul flew. I felt the same way when I was with Mother. But when he looked away, no longer seeing me, I felt cold. Like I was in an Indian summer, and the reality of winter had set in.

Conversation seemed endless. We talked about all kinds of things from politics to religions to cartoons. I found myself spilling my heart out, telling him the deep dark secrets of my soul. It was like my past was an attic and I was climbing up the stairs with Jimmy, swinging the door wide open to a room filled with cobwebs and spiders.

He told me of his life. How he was seventeen years old and his parents had been divorced the past eleven years. How his girlfriend had ripped his heart in two.

I felt pangs of jealousy at the thought of another girl holding his thoughts and his hand as I did now. It slipped away into pity when his voice became shaky. His eyes were brown, filled with a mixture of love and pain, calling out to me. They reminded me of a Basset Hound with large brown eyes so full of soul that you couldn't help falling in love. I wanted somebody to love me so much it hurt.

"Listen," he said, "I have to work tomorrow too. But could I see you later, same time, same place?"

I nodded, unable to speak past the catch in my throat. I was in love with a boy I had just met, who was two years older than me. And he liked me.

"Yes," I whispered.

I got back to Whispering Pines after dark. The family was playing a game, and laughter floated out the window. Their profiles were silhouetted through the window by a corner lamp. They seemed so happy, so complete. I didn't belong with them. I used the back door, slipping inside. They didn't notice when the door stuck, and I had to slam it shut. They didn't notice much of anything, so engrossed were they in their happiness. I avoided the creaky stair on my way up.

The moment I reached my room, I flew to my desk. I turned the pages of my journal to the next blank one—so white and creamy, perfect for my words. My passions poured out through the spout that was my pen.

*These eyes, so brown,*
*Deep into I fall,*
*The smile, so sweet,*
*I cannot see.*
*But you, your touch,*
*Gentle as the fresh spring rain,*
*Lasting as all time,*
*You, inside, you set me free.*

## Chapter Eight

Footsteps.

Loud angry ones marched through the house on a mission. Mimi's footsteps. I could tell the footsteps of the Burtons apart. John's were heavy and slow, resounding of stability and respectability. Anna's, petite and soft, always seemed afraid of breaking something. Ricky's were quick. He walked without caring where his feet fell. Mimi's were loud and, for the most part, angry.

"What the hell do you think you're doing?"

She hit the screen door so hard it made a black mark on the side of the house. I looked up from my book, a mystery thriller by S. Birch, and put my feet down on the porch to steady the swing.

"What are you talking about?"

"You know what I'm talking about."

But I didn't. I wondered what I had done this time to be the subject of her wrath. Her face glowed bright red like a cherry tomato.

"Jimmy. Jimmy Boswell. The boy *I* like! The one who was going to be *my* boyfriend!"

Now I understood. At the beach, the boy she had a crush on was Jimmy. I could understand why. After all, what girl wouldn't like him. But he was way too old for her. And he liked *me*.

"He's not your boyfriend, and he never will be. He wouldn't notice such a baby."

"He was going to be mine. You ruined my life. You ruin everything. Dad and Mom always argued because of you. We had almost become a normal family, and then you showed up. You wrecked everything. I hate you. I wish you were dead!"

Tears streamed down her cheeks. She choked on each breath she inhaled. She turned around and smacked into the door, wrenching it open to run inside like she couldn't stand to share the same air with me anymore.

I sat as though paralyzed. I was not responsible for breaking up a nonexistent relationship between Mimi and Jimmy. But I had ruined the family. My disappearance tore them apart, and when the wound was healing, I reopened it again. I didn't ask to be a part of this family. I hated everyone in it, with the exception of Ricky.

Sweet little Ricky. He was only nine years old. John and Anna tried to force him to fill the hole I'd made in their family. He'd almost succeeded in making them forget. Almost.

Footsteps again. This time they were quiet, so quiet I almost didn't hear them. Anna pushed open the door, frowning at the black mark.

"John won't like that," she said to the house. "John won't like that at all."

She stood by the swing, looking awkward and seeming unsure of whether she should sit down by me. She did, but on the very edge, hunched over and ready to flee should I make the slightest move. She was no doubt less afraid of spiders.

"Do you hate me?" I blurted it out, unable to stop myself.

She sat very still, as though considering her words.

"Yes. And myself."

"Why?"

How can anyone hate her daughter? She contemplated my face before answering.

"You were my firstborn, my little baby girl. It isn't the same with mothers as it is for fathers. We have a bond with our children that a man could never have. I fed you at my breast, sang lullabies to put you to sleep. You were such a good baby. You didn't cry very much."

Anna stopped, as if revealing that she once loved me more than anything was painful to her. I knew it hurt me.

"We had Miami when you were two years old. She was a different sort of child, loud and opinionated. So different from you. While you would play by yourself, she couldn't be left alone for five minutes. She doesn't like the name Miami, you know. She says it makes her sound like white trash. She only answers to Mimi."

Her thoughts seemed to have wandered, and she took a moment to collect herself. This was the woman who loved me before anyone else did. This was the woman who crooned to her belly in anticipation. Who taught me my first words and witnessed my first steps.

"You were five, and Mimi was two. We were in Shop 'N' Save. You were upset because I wouldn't buy you a chocolate bar. I reached for a box of Cheerios, put it in the cart, looked up, and you were gone. You had disappeared. I started to call out your name, walking up and down the aisles. I thought you had just wandered away. Then I started to panic, and I went to Customer Service. They kept paging your name. You didn't come. So the manager called the police and had clerks stand by the doors in case you tried to go outside. They searched that whole store, and you weren't there. The police even brought in dogs to sniff you out. No one remembered seeing you leave, not even after I showed them pictures. Not even after I described your new pink coat. You were so proud of that coat."

Again she was silent, and I could see the years melting away. Anna was once more the frantic young mother who had lost her baby in a grocery store. The lines of worry had just begun to show, and the lines of age were not far behind. I helped to paint on the lines.

"John hated me for losing you. I hated myself for losing you. And I hated you most of all. What had I done to deserve such treatment? What have I done?"

Anna's voice rose in pitch as she started getting hysterical, raising her hands up to the sky. Tears filled her voice. She wasn't hunched over anymore.

"What have I done to deserve this life?"

And she looked at me. "I will always hate you."

That slap from the words didn't hurt as much as the pain inside, knowing that the woman who'd once loved me didn't anymore. Anna had carried me for nine long months and spent hours bringing me into the world. But she wasn't my mother. She hadn't raised me in sunshine, protected by a wreath of love. My mother was in jail somewhere in Massachusetts. Anna was a shell of a woman, a fragile husk whose features bore the imprint of a woman named Anna Burton who had lived fifteen years ago. Anna was dead inside already. Who knew when the outside would follow?

## Chapter Nine

*O Mighty River*
*With rapids and waves*
*Long smooth stretches*
*Warm summer days*
*Storm clouds they gather*
*The darkness begins*
*My soul is so heavy*
*I long to dive in*
*And then they part*
*The sun now does smile*
*Perhaps I might stay*
*For a little while*

It was after midnight. I had seen Jimmy earlier. We'd walked and talked for over two hours. I didn't remember a word of the conversation except for those three...

"I love you."

After that my ears went deaf, and the sun shone brighter than ever. My first kiss happened straight from a romance novel. It was light and sweet and honey-coated. It was blizzards in December, soft April rain, the shade of a tree in August, the intense New England hues of September. I couldn't remember a moment so perfect in my life. Jimmy didn't care that my life was messed up. He didn't care that Mother was in jail, that Anna hated me. He didn't care about any of that. Jimmy just wanted to be with me.

"I'm going to Vermont for two weeks to see my Dad. You'll still be here, right?" He asked me.

"Yes. I'll be here. And I'll be waiting for you."

"Okay." He grinned.

"Okay."

We both burst out laughing at the absurdity of it all. Then his hands were gripping mine, the calluses rough against my skin. His eyes were deep, and I was falling in. We leaned towards each other, his breath warm on my cheek. His lips were both soft and hard at the same time. I couldn't breathe, I couldn't move, I couldn't think. I was lost in a sea of colors, each more radiant than the last.

I would have written a poem, but all my words had deserted me. I felt drained, without the simple strength to pick up my pen.

"Mary?"

Only one person in this family called me Mary. The only one who called me by any name.

"What's wrong, Ricky?"

He pushed open the door, trembling in the doorway.

"I had a nightmare."

"Why don't you sleep with me tonight?"

The bed wasn't big enough for two, but he ran in the room and snuggled into it anyway. He seemed both surprised and relieved that I didn't turn him away.

"Why didn't you wake up...your mom?" I asked him.

His face screwed up and turned into a look of unease. He picked invisible lint off the comforter, refusing to meet my eyes.

"She doesn't wake up. She takes these pills every night so she can sleep, and she doesn't wake up till morning. Sometimes she drinks stuff too. Only when Daddy's not here.

Tuesday she shut the door and drank a whole bottle. I saw it in the morning. When she drinks, she doesn't get up till really late, and I have to make my own breakfast."

I was shocked, but tried not to show it. "Well, you can sleep with me tonight."

"Okay."

We were pressed so close together I was afraid of hurting him. I laid my left arm on my chest so it wouldn't dangle off the bed.

"Mary?"

"Mmm-hmm?"

"Did you know that Aunt Joey is coming for the Fourth of July? She's the best."

"No, I didn't, Ricky. I've never heard of an Aunt Joey."

"Night, Mary."

"Good night, Ricky."

## Chapter Ten

Aunt Joey was slender and as tall as her brother, John. They shared the same dirty brown hair and hazel eyes. John's face always appeared sharp, as though he were sitting on a knife and in pain, but too stubborn to move. Aunt Joey had a narrow face too, but hers seemed broad and sunny.

I was washing the dishes at the sink. Ricky was drying. Mimi was off at Lana's house, her home away from home. John pulled into the driveway. You could always tell it was him because he drove fast down the street, then slammed on the brakes to pull in. And out of the car popped a circus clown. She wore purple jeans and a bright orange and yellow sweatshirt with a red lightning bolt dividing the two colors down the middle. Her glasses were green rimmed, with rose colored lenses. Her smile could have swallowed up Whispering Pines.

"You must be Madonna!" she exclaimed. "We've all missed you. I was in Tuscany, so I couldn't visit as soon as I wanted to. Sorry, kiddo."

"Actually, it's Mary."

She didn't miss a beat.

"Mary it is then. How're you doing, kiddo?"

"Um…I'm fine."

"Ha! Fine, good, okay, that's what everybody says. I want to find the one person in the world who actually tells the truth.

I can't wait to ask him, 'how are you doing?' and have the guy tell me he's never felt worse. Honesty, kiddo, that's the ticket. What this world needs is a lot more honesty."

Then she whirled into the house, leaving me in her wake. Hurricane Joey had just passed through the area.

Aunt Joey decided that she was going to take us kids to a great lobster place she knew. She told Anna and John to 'enjoy their time alone together.' She had the keys to John's car before he could voice any protests, and we were out the door.

We stopped at Lana's house, honking the horn at the gray structure. Mimi came running out, surprised but with a smile. Lana lingered behind, shy for once.

"What's the matter, kiddo?" Aunt Joey asked her. "You don't like lobster?"

Lana climbed in the car too.

It was about a twenty-five minute drive away, and Aunt Joey had AC/DC blasting the whole way there. The air streaming through all the open windows ruffled our hair. She honked the horn and waved at everyone we passed, people looking up and smiling, some waving back.

"Do you know all those people?" I asked her.

"Nope, not a single one. But that's not the point, now is it? You should always be friendly. Don't have to be waving only at your friends. If you don't reach out to anyone else, how're you going to meet anyone new?"

I couldn't argue with her logic. Hadn't complete chance, a small accident, and a few words brought Jimmy and me together?

We passed white farmhouses with sprawling fields, shoots of new plants already poking through the ground in even rows. Cows dotted verdant green pastures. Old barns, seeming ready to crumble at any moment, were strewn throughout. An old man walked his dog on the edge of the road. The sun glinted off his bald spot, and when he smiled, I saw he was missing a lot of his teeth.

Mimi and Lana started to giggle, the mean sort of giggle they had for dorky-looking people. Aunt Joey gave them a sharp look.

"That old geezer's got one hundred times more brains and sense than the two of you put together. A life that long and full, that's a beautiful thing."

Mimi's lips moved in the rearview mirror. "That's a beautiful thing."

Lana laughed at her, hand over mouth. Aunt Joey didn't seem to notice or to care.

"We're here."

*Here* was Two Lights. Twin lighthouses sat within easy walking distance of each other. The one on the left teetered too close to the edge of a rocky cliff. The one on the right was perched on a glossy green hill.

We parked to the right in a dirt parking lot. Rock stairs led upwards to a grassy flat area sprinkled with twelve picnic tables. Each one had a red and white Coca-Cola sun umbrella. The restaurant was small with no indoor seating, only a screened window to order through. I thought it was adorable.

Aunt Joey said she would order for us. I walked toward the sea, to where the grass stopped and the ground took a sharp fall. Flat rocks stretched for ten yards or so, the waves lapping at the farthest ones. The rest sheltered seagulls and a few tide pools.

We feasted on lobster dipped in butter and French fries. I'd never eaten lobster before, but the claim that Maine lobsters take the prize as the best in the world must be true.

Using metal pincers to crush the shell the way Aunt Joey showed me, I cracked open the claws to get at the meat. Then I sucked the juices out of the legs, popping them off one by one. I had to snap the tail off by bending it in the wrong direction. To split open the middle, I put my hands under the body and pressed against the sides. Part of the tail meat had greenish-colored stuff in it, which I didn't eat. Aunt Joey did.

"It's a delicacy," she said, smacking her lips.

Butter ran down our chins, sliding down the plastic lobster bibs and into our laps. Everyone was equal when eating lobster. We got messy and slippery, and no one cared. We were all laughing, even Mimi and Lana, a warm laughter as rich as lobster. The kind of laugh that Mother had. It warmed me up down to my toes.

During the car ride back, Aunt Joey asked if I had ever seen the Fourth of July Parade.

"The whole town turns out for it. It's a great time. All the little kiddies decorate their bikes and ride in it, and people dress up and throw candy. Plus all the floats are homemade, and the volunteer fire department drives the trucks with the lights and sirens running." She sounded excited.

That night I dreamt I decorated my bike and ran Anna over with it.

## Chapter Eleven

The parade was everything Aunt Joey had promised and more. We stood in front of the Temple to watch, along with what seemed to be the entire town. Aunt Joey looked like she had dressed up to march in it, not just be a spectator. Whole families wore identical outfits. Little kids zoomed by on their tricycles. All the floats were made by families and friends. People on roller blades threw candy. A man on stilts had dressed up as Uncle Sam. One group of about twenty carried beach chairs and did a song and dance routine, and a Dober-man pulled a beautiful little wooden cart in which a terrier rode.

All the parades in my memory were loud and obnoxious. They involved standing around for hours on a crowded city street in the freezing cold or in a heat wave to watch for five minutes. This one was loud, but it carried a good feeling. Everyone in Ocean Park wore red, white, and blue and came out to celebrate with flags. After the parade was over, all the participants received rocket popsicles. A band played patri-otic tunes next to the pavilion while the mayor and town coun-cil presented awards for the best decorated bikes.

Aunt Joey and I walked to the beach to see the sand cas-tle competition. Plots staked out with colored ribbons held characters and designs made out of sand. I saw The Little Mermaid, a beach dude in an inner tube, a car, pirate ship, and sand castles galore. All done by amateurs, many of them were sprayed with colored water. The beach was crowded even for a Saturday morning, people oohing and aahing over the sand sculptures. Prizes were awarded—sand shovels painted bronze, silver, and gold.

Sandals in hand, we walked barefoot to the ice cream parlor. It was crowded with people standing elbow to arm to side. Aunt Joey bought me a moose tracks ice cream cone, vanilla ice cream with chocolate and Reese's chunks in it. We crossed the street to the small Ocean Park library and sat on the benches in the middle of the lawn.

"It must be hard for you, trying to adjust to a new family, a new life."

"Yeah."

I didn't tell her how I would never adjust to this family. I didn't want to talk about Mother.

"Your mother, the one who took you, was wrong in what she did. But from what I can see, she brought you up right."

I didn't say anything. Aunt Joey had just praised the woman who had stolen me from my rightful parents. Or was she praising me? I wondered a lot about Mother. Did she take me because she loved me, or did she take me to have something to love?

Aunt Joey asked what I thought of her brother.

"John?" The surprise in my voice was evident. "He's, he's…"

"Stuck up, bossy, controlling, annoying, narrow minded, and pig headed. He also lies." She smiled at me. "I should know. I had to live with him for sixteen years. And your mom, Anna, she's something else. But I love Mimi and Ricky like nothing else in the world. That's why I keep coming back to see them. I would die for those kids. I would even live for them. Living is much harder than dying."

An unexpected ally. I was drawn to Aunt Joey. She reminded me of Mother, a thought that hit like a sledgehammer. Both had an unconditional capacity for love.

"Ricky says you write poetry."

That wasn't expected either, a statement and not a question. We were now walking back to Whispering Pines, the trees' shade cooling the tar beneath our feet. I carried my sandals in one hand, the remains of a triple scoop ice cream cone in another.

"Yes, but it's not real poetry. It doesn't rhyme all the time, and the meter's off. But it's me, a reflection of myself."

"I'd like to hear one."

For the second time in my life I found myself sharing a secret with someone else. For the second time I was opening the door and letting the light shine in.

She sat on my bed, the comforter bunching under her weight. She inspected my room with a wise eye while I dug out my journal. The only decoration I had added was the small jar of sea glass on my desk, already spilling over. I was going to have to get another one.

"You really should decorate the place, kiddo. It's a bit…"

"Boring?"

"Cold."

An interesting choice of words. I held out the journal for her inspection. She insisted that I read one to her. She closed her eyes, taking a deep breath and exhaling in a slow, precise way, like she was meditating.

> *My soul is shattered,*
> *My heart in pieces,*
> *My mind laid low,*
> *In the dirt.*
> *But from this I will rise,*
> *A glorious flower,*
> *A phoenix from its dusty doom.*
> *With ivory wings will I soar*
> *And smile at you.*

Aunt Joey didn't say anything. She just sat there with her eyes closed. I was fidgeting, digging my fingernails hard enough into my arms to draw blood. It trickled down my arms. All I could think was, "What if she hates it? What if she thinks it's stupid or childish?"

Then her eyes peeked open. Her mouth parted wide.

"That was beautiful."

## Chapter Twelve

"That was beautiful. That was beautiful." Those heavenly words resounded through my head.

John took Aunt Joey to the airport in Portland last night on his way to Manchester for another week's work. Before she left, she held me close in a bear hug.

"Dance crazy in the moonlight," she'd whispered into my ear.

When I asked what that meant, she smiled and said it was the meaning of life.

The car inched backward out of the driveway, John looking over his shoulder so as not to hit anything. It was funny how he sped to the place he hated, but crept away from it.

"Wait!" I'd called. "What does Joey stand for?"

"Josephine!" she'd yelled back, "but I hate that name!"

I was in my new bathing suit, a string bikini, red with white tropical flowers. Aunt Joey bought it for me, saying that I was fifteen years old and should look that way. For the first time since I had arrived here, I felt attractive. So when Anna didn't get up in the morning and Mimi and Ricky were playing video games, I walked to the beach.

The tide was washing out, and people crowded the area. They thinned out as I walked along the wet sands to the right. Homes lined the waterfront, and there were no lifeguards.

Sporadic groups of people dotted the beach here. I passed the craggy rocks that rose from the sea, rearing their backs from below the waves to reveal treasures hidden in their pools. Kids with neon colored buckets and LL Bean swimsuits picked up crabs and starfish and broken pieces of shells while their moms admired their finds.

This was where I always turned around, but something compelled me to keep going.

I walked and walked and walked, my eyes focused on the ground. As each wave slipped around my feet and fell back, the sand glistened and sparkled as if it were filled with tiny diamonds. Black onyx-colored specks created intricate patterns beneath my feet. The small bag I had with me held a notebook and several handfuls of sea glass. It bumped against my leg every step or so.

I must have walked for over a mile before rounding the natural corner of the beach. The jetty in the distance pointed its long rocky finger in the direction of happiness. I walked until I couldn't, then climbed up flat slabs of gray rocks until my feet hit the street. I didn't put on my sandals.

A red convertible full of college boys drove by me, going the opposite direction.

"Nice butt!" one of them yelled.

"Thanks!" I yelled back. What was I supposed to say to a comment like that?

I walked down the road, passing several seafood restaurants before taking a left. The tar gave way to sand, then concrete, and then I was on the jetty. It was made of gray rocks heaped up on top of one another, each with at least one man-made flat side. A lonely man in khaki shorts sat off to one side, his fishing pole in front of him and his trusty Lab beside him.

Making my way out to him, hands splayed against a fall, I saw that he wasn't that old, maybe in his late forties.

"Good morning," he said.

"I think it's good afternoon now."

"A-yuh," he said.

That strange two syllable word New Englanders use could express doubt, anger, compliance, sarcasm, or agree with you at any time or in any combination. The meaning was determined by the tone of the speaker. I understood his response to indicate agreement, that it was a good afternoon.

I walked further down until the smooth rocks gave way to sharp and pointy ones. Then I pulled out my half-finished letter to Jimmy, sitting on the last flat rock. In it I poured out my heart about Aunt Joey, the parade, and my love for him. But it wasn't complete; it lacked something.

The words formed in my mind, pen moving on paper without the hand realizing what it was doing.

*A picture's worth a thousand words,*
*For you I'd write a book,*
*And word for word copy a library,*
*No matter how long it took.*
*Ten thousand pens, a forest of paper,*
*For you I'd have the best,*
*And love you sweetly, dearly, truly,*
*'Til you were laid to rest.*

## Chapter Thirteen

Mimi and I made pancakes. Anna hadn't come out of her room in the last three days. No one had talked to her. We watched Ricky and took him to the beach. Mimi made tuna fish sandwiches and grilled cheese. I made spaghetti and cooked a chicken. We had enough chicken for two days' worth of meals. The trays we put in front of Anna's doors would disappear for a day, and then reappear in the hallway, looking as though they hadn't been touched.

I didn't fight with Mimi at all. It was as if a dark fog had descended on the house, and we couldn't get enough air. Lana came over and said it was like the air in a crypt. She was a charming girl.

Mimi was pouring more batter into the pan when the phone rang. Once, twice. Its shrillness cut the air like a knife. We stared at the yellow appliance in silence. No one called Whispering Pines, not unless something bad had happened or John couldn't make it up for the weekend again. It rang a third time. Mimi, spatula raised in her hand like a shield, moved to pick it up. She froze as we heard a reedy voice talking from upstairs. It was Anna using the phone in her bedroom. John had one put in up there in case he needed to take an emergency call.

Then there was silence, the creaking of the floor above us, and the fog descended. We ate the pancakes in silence. I finished only half of mine because it stuck to my throat. Even Ricky felt the tension, which was worse than the first night we had dinner together. He asked if he could go outside and walked out the door when I nodded. Even his footsteps echoed sorrow.

The shower upstairs was running. Mimi and I sat at the table, watching the maple syrup congeal with the butter on our plates. It was real Vermont maple syrup, not the fake stuff. John was raised on real maple syrup.

Footsteps echoed on the stairs. Mimi raised one eyebrow. It was like a horror movie, where you could hear death coming and there was nowhere to run.

Anna's feet cleared the bottom step, and I could see her face. It had grown sharp and gaunt, without any expression. She gestured towards the door.

"Get Ricky. Great-grandma died. Pack your bags."

Then she shuffled over to the fridge, pulling it open. Her sundress was as faded as her soul, and was missing a button in the back. Mimi didn't move. Neither did I. We sat there in shock. I'd never met my great-grandma, and now I would never get the chance.

Anna turned back to face us, orange juice in hand.

"Didn't you hear me? I said move!" she screamed in a hoarse voice.

We moved.

## Chapter Fourteen.

My first funeral was not what I expected. We went to the funeral parlor all dressed up to show respect for someone who wasn't even there to see it. The wake was the worst part.

The woman lying in her casket wore a blue suit and clutched an ivory rosary. I wondered how her fingers were made to stick together. She was pale, though not as white as I thought she'd be, and looked like an exhibit from Madame Tussaud's.

A little bench padded with a crimson cushion sat in front of the casket. John pushed at the small of my back so I would kneel down with him. I was so close to her, I could count the minute hairs on her chin. John closed his eyes, seeming to pray. Since I didn't believe in God, I just studied the wax-like figure of my great-grandmother.

We got up and walked around the room. At every clump of people, John would stop and introduce me as his daughter, Madonna. To myself, I said my name was Mary. Aloud, I said nothing.

Some people were crying, but most talked of how good it was that she had been put out of her suffering. Why was dying considered a good thing? Was it good to be lying in a coffin, unable to enjoy the flowers or the relatives she had never known? Then I heard Aunt Joey's voice inside my head. *Living is a lot harder than dying.*

The next day, temperatures soared into the nineties. The humidity made my blue dress stick to my legs. Sweat stains appeared under Ricky's arms, darkening his white shirt. I couldn't tell with John because he wore a suit. The church didn't have air conditioning.

Old women in black skirts and white blouses with little red capes hanging off one shoulder brought the casket in, rolling it down the aisle. They belonged to the same organization my great-grandmother had, the Sisters of the Holy something or other. Ricky fidgeted beside me. Anna stared at me, her dark eyes meeting mine, but there didn't seem to be anything behind her eyes. It startled me until I realized that, while she was looking right at me, she didn't see me. She could have been staring at a blank wall for all she noticed.

The eulogy was given a quarter in French, a quarter in English, and the other half in tears. The speaker spoke of Norma's goodness, love, and devotion. Of the way she used to knit socks on the front porch and keep chickens in the garage and of the time at a family reunion when she set Uncle Ronnie's toupee on fire. She droned on for the better part of an hour.

Then we followed the procession out of the church and into our cars. The little purple flags on the car hoods proclaimed us members of a funeral. As the members of this exclusive club, we got to bypass all the other traffic and drive through red lights, traveling in a long caravan.

The grave was all ready when we arrived. Flowers from the funeral home were placed around the coffin. People gathered in little groups, talking in low tones as though the dead would be offended by a normal tone of voice. We all were waiting, and I had to ask Mimi for what. She shot me an "aren't you stupid" look before answering.

However, the priest who was supposed to come never showed up. Maybe because he was from Quebec and spoke little English, he got lost. Or maybe no one would give him a ride. Perhaps he was never told to go to the cemetery by one of the few French-speaking relatives. At any rate, it was obvious he didn't plan to make an appearance.

It also became apparent my family wouldn't let insignificant details ruin an otherwise good funeral. The same Uncle Ronnie whose toupee had been set on fire borrowed a Bible from one of the funeral guys and proceeded to read. He read a part about David and his slingshot, a paragraph about love, and finished up with Jesus turning water into wine. I guessed that he was picking passages at random.

When he finished reading, he crossed the air with his Bible, and then all present crossed themselves. The formalities over, I watched in shock as the relatives made off with bits and pieces of the funeral bouquets. The lady wasn't even in the ground, and already they were taking her belongings.

But the worst was yet to come. All present were invited to a lunch at the Wellsley Conference Center in remembrance.

For a bunch of people who had just been at a funeral a mere twenty minutes before, they had big appetites and cheery dispositions. Random adults would ask me whose daughter I was, and gasp when I told them. They all wanted to know what it felt like to be kidnapped. As I was five at the time, I couldn't remember. After talking to me, every one of them would say it was a good thing I was home again, then walk away talking to one another.

Home again? Home wasn't Whispering Pines. Home wasn't in Manchester. Home was with a woman in a jail cell, who probably shared said cell with someone named Honey or Bubbles or Slit-your-throat-Sue.

The room buzzed with the energy of the Burton family. They talked like there was no tomorrow, drank like the pending return of the Prohibition, and laughed like rabid hyenas. Ricky disappeared to join in a game of tag.

A woman in a purple pantsuit walked right up to me. I almost screamed in surprise, she looked so much like Aunt

Joey. Closer inspection showed that her outfit was too expensive, her hair too permed, and her nails too long.

"I'm your Aunt Jane," she said, sticking out a manicured hand. The only calluses present must have come from filing her nails.

"I'm Mary."

"Mmm-hmm. You look surprised. Bet Joey didn't tell you about me. And John never would. That's brotherly love for you. There are three of us, you know. Used to be four, but Jacob ran off to Tibet with some Chinese girl, and we haven't heard from him since. Welcome to the Burton Family."

Like Aunt Joey, Aunt Jane had a strong personality. Unlike Aunt Joey, she grated on my nerves. I wished she would pick someone else to talk at.

"So you're the little girl Anna lost. And that trash that stole you is rotting in jail while Anna falls apart now that you're back. Anna's not much of a woman, is she?" Aunt Jane chuckled as though she'd just divulged some inside joke.

I didn't laugh. My belly squeezed itself into knots, and my fists doubled up so tight that my fingernails dug into my palms. Aunt Jane didn't notice, just kept on talking and talking. I stared at her lips, but didn't see them move. I just heard her whine in my ears, buzzing like an annoying bee. She started to laugh, her head thrown back, her mouth open. A giant chunk of broccoli was wedged between her front teeth. She leaned forward, the sight of the broccoli breaking me out of my trance.

"Now, honey, you be smart like me. A couple of years, then you find yourself a rich old guy. Marry him and play the devoted wife till he croaks on you. Sure his kids will put up a fight, but you'll get most of the money anyway."

She tossed her curls and grinned.

"You have a piece of broccoli between your teeth," I said. Then I escaped.

## Chapter Fifteen

The silver lady was still there when I got back. I wondered if she had noticed that I was gone. The tide was high now, but she still combed the sand. That golden, fluffy stuff didn't hold any treasures, at least none that I could see. But that didn't stop the silver lady.

The next afternoon, and the following afternoon, she still walked the shoreline. I brought a book instead, settling down on the sand, letting the warmth of the sun's rays heat my body and soothe my aching heart. Jimmy would be back in four days.

I spent as much time reading the new thriller by S. Birch as I did watching the silver lady. In it, a man was killing cancer patients by lethal injections, but nobody knew they were homicides. I had just gotten to the part where he kills the cop's wife who had breast cancer when a shadow fell across the page. It belonged to the silver lady, who spread open her hands. In them was a small piece of indigo blue sea glass, so small I had to squint to see it.

"You see, it's easy to walk right over life's little joys. You have to stoop down and watch out for them, or else they'll just pass you by."

Then she smiled, her teeth glossy and straight. Her right hand dipped into her back pocket. It pulled out a folded piece of notebook paper.

"I write poetry, too."

She dropped the folded paper at my feet and walked decisively past me. Knowing what I would see, I didn't turn to watch her go—the silver lining of a cloud walking off a golden beach.

I unfolded the piece of paper. It was sticking to itself from the salt of the ocean. On it, in black, curly writing, was a small letter.

*Dear girl,*

*I see you alone. I watch you more than you can know, not just when you're picking up sea glass up at my side, but during the day when you walk alone. I saw you with that boy. I saw you with your little brother. I know your story. Word gets around fast in a small town, even when you're alone as I am. What I'm trying to say, though not very successfully, is that no matter what happens to you, don't give in to hatred.*

> *An eclipse of the sun,*
> *The roses lay dying,*
> *The bird's sweet song no more.*
> *Like a plague does it come,*
> *Burning black,*
> *Blacker than the darkest night,*
> *Blacker than the murderer's soul.*
> *You cannot shield your eyes from darkness,*
> *Cannot ignore the raging fire.*
> *So why do you not see,*
> *This world is dying*
> *From hate?*

*Love, Sylvia.*

## Chapter Sixteen

"Hey baby."

I didn't think anyone's arms could be so strong and warm and loving. He crushed me to his chest, while I groped wildly at his back, clutching at his shirt. Our lips crashed together like waves upon the rocks. I always thought love at first sight was a myth, a joke. But I was experiencing it, living the dream. His scent filled my nostrils, musky and sweet and Jimmy. I could have died happy right then. Then his lips began to form those three words I'd imagined him saying so many times. And, and…

I woke up alone in my room. Reality hit like a freight train. Jimmy would not be home until tomorrow. My heart pounded from the intensity of the dream. Although no soft rays peeked through my window, I got up anyway. Sleep had become a hopeless cause.

Sylvia had promised to take me to the flea market today. When we met, neither of us mentioned the letter or the poem. It was as though she had never written those words, as though she'd never had those thoughts and put them to paper. A silent pact had been made, a secret understanding. I didn't ask for anything more.

Aunt Joey and Sylvia were pen pals. I hadn't even known they were aware of each other's existence. Aunt Joey had never mentioned anything to me. Sylvia had to be much older than Aunt Joey. I couldn't see them being friends from college. She never told me how they had met, but I suspected that Aunt Joey had been the starting force in their friendship.

Sylvia said that she lived alone and liked being that way. But she watched the people on the beach, and that gave her entire families to belong to. The Pitrowski family next door, she said, was expecting a baby, but they hadn't told their two teenage daughters yet. Marge Anderson was having a love affair with one of the lifeguards. She said that I knew who he was, the only red-haired one on the beach. They would smile in passing during the day, but at night they had romantic dinners by candlelight and professed their undying love for each other. In my mind I'd already called the lifeguard Freckles O'Riley because of his face and hair. Sylvia said his name was Bob Johnson.

"Then there's Dom Merrigan," she'd said. "He goes fishing almost every day, rain or shine. Just sits on the jetty with his chocolate Lab beside him. The dog's name is Butch, and he is as blind as the proverbial bat."

Sylvia's knowledge seemed to encompass just about everyone in Ocean Park. She knew my family. I had finally come to terms with the fact that the Burtons were, in fact, my family. No matter what they said to me, or what they did to me, they were a part of me. Like silver strands in the spider's web, we were separate and individual, yet pieces of the same puzzle.

Sylvia knew all about Anna's depression. I had never thought of her as being depressed. Depression was such a cold, final word, a door that slammed shut on your fingers. If one were sad, one could become happy again; if *she* were down, *she* could rise back up. But depression was a pit that couldn't be climbed out of. The sides were just to steep, the rocks too slippery to get a good grip on.

It made sense though—the pills, the drinking, the vacant looks on her face. John seemed almost always annoyed with her. Only in rare moments did they demonstrate any happiness together. I'd believed that he was never in Maine because he had to work. But he'd called again to say he just couldn't make it up this weekend, and could we please forgive him. Then I realized he couldn't stand to be near her.

I took a long, warm shower, running my fingers slowly over my scalp, massaging in the fruity suds. Mimi was sleeping over at Lana's again, and Ricky was at some friend's house. It was the first sleepover he'd been to all summer. I think some well-meaning mother had caught on to Anna's problems and thought she would do her a favor and get Ricky out of her hair. The only one receiving the favor was me since I had to watch him most days. Anna either slept in or just never got up.

In the kitchen the cupboards were almost bare. I could see the patterns of the wood on the back walls of them. The one over the sink had a spider web in the corner. I shut the door; I hate spiders. I ended up eating leftover Spaghetti O's, last night's dinner. I ate them cold, not bothering with the microwave. The sliminess made me gag, but I didn't care.

The sun peeked through the tree tops, the slight chill of the night air dissipating in the morning warmth. Sylvia was going to pick me up in her car. I hadn't been in a vehicle since Aunt Joey and the trip to Two Lights. I felt strange getting into her car after she pulled into the driveway. Drawing the seat belt across my chest and clicking it in the receiver felt like a foreign action. We drove through side streets, passing houses that were just beginning to wake up. Most were summer homes like Whispering Pines, filled with laughter and sunshine only during the summer months or on weekends. Despite the differences in design, the beach chairs and Frisbees, coolers, shovels, and brightly colored plastic buckets lying in the yards connected them all.

The flea market was in full swing when we pulled up, the small patch of dirt allocated for parking brimming with cars.

A brown and yellow restaurant across the street charged three dollars to park in the lawn near their matching cabins. We paid the boy and crossed the street with the other merry customers.

All flea markets are unique, no two ever the same. This one had rows of tables lined up, most shaded by white half-tents. Merchandise was arranged on embroidered tablecloths and special wooden cases, or sometimes on the chipped picnic tables. Sylvia carried a canvas bag with baby handprints stamped on it in primary colors. It was for our purchases. She would pick something up—a clip or a wooden spoon or a shirt—examining it, her lips pursed and eyes squinting. The crow's feet around her eyes stood out when she was studying someone's crochet work.

We passed a Barbie-blond who sat in a worn blue folding chair. She looked almost artificial, bronzed and faded from too much tanning and not enough protection. Her body's remains spoke of a time past when it could have made some men cry and others kill. She picked at the frayed edges of the chair, seeming unwilling to meet anyone's eyes. Behind her, dozens of beautiful paintings sat on easels or lined the back of the tent. One seascape called out to me. It appeared to have been painted at dusk, the waves lapping at the sand. The sun cast its honey glow on the beach while the ocean looked calm and cool. A lone figure stood off to the left, staring out across the water, the waves shuffling around her feet. It contributed to the beauty and was surrounded by it in turn. Though her back was turned, her hair and her stance identified her.

The figure was me.

Sylvia's breath warmed my left ear.

"It's you," she said. "It's you on the beach."

"Yes."

I wanted that picture more than I'd ever wanted anything. The Barbie woman didn't respond the first time I asked for the price, so I raised my voice a little louder.

"How much for this painting?"

She got up, pushing against the chair like an old woman. But she couldn't have been over forty. Shuffling over, she tilted her head up slightly, looking at it through her eyelashes. I couldn't tell what color her eyes were.

"Fifty dollars."

Her gaze moved back down to that spot between her feet she found so fascinating. I didn't have fifty dollars. Well, I did, but it was John's money, and I couldn't spend it on a painting. Sylvia watched me turn and walk away. I heard her voice behind me.

"Will you take forty?"

"A-yuh," Barbie agreed.

I returned to the tent in time to see the deal struck, hands shaken, and money exchanged. The Barbie woman shuffled back to her chair, stiffly bending to pick up a bag. She shuffled back, scuffing her feet in the dirt, then wrapped the picture in yellowed tissue paper before putting it in the plastic bag. She handed it to Sylvia, who handed it to me.

I planned to hang it on my wall opposite the bed. I was sure a hammer and nails were lying around Whispering Pines somewhere. I would wake each morning and view the perfection that was the day I stood upon the sand and gazed into the sea.

The Barbie woman never looked up. When we drove back down the street, I saw her in her chair, picking at the edges with one hand, still staring at the same spot between her toes.

I couldn't believe that Sylvia had bought the painting for me. Why would she do that? She barely knew me.

"That was really nice of you to get the picture. You didn't have to, you know."

"I know," she said, a small smile passing across her lips. "And you're welcome."

We rode on in comfortable silence.

## Chapter Seventeen

*If you and I could fly,*
*And soar above the clouds,*
*If one should choose to die,*
*Could the other then be found?*

"Let's walk to the pier," he said.

That was no dream. Jimmy had come back, and we had fallen into each other's arms, an experience unparalleled by a figment of my imagination. He told me about spending all his time at Lake Champlain on his Dad's boat, missing me.

"I would've written, but that would have made me miss you even more."

We walked hand in hand for all to see, just like the couples I had detested at the beginning of the summer. Anna had dragged herself to the beach, where she dozed in the sun. Ricky was content in the tide pools, creating lives for his plastic animals.

While many other couples held hands as they walked to the pier, I felt like we were the only ones there. We were the only couple truly in love, the only ones that mattered. I supposed all couples felt this way.

The pier stretched out into the water, the street from the land running right up to it where a wooden ramp led to the pier proper. Stairs reached up from the beach below, hidden in among the thick poles holding the whole thing up. They looked like giant pieces of driftwood, as if a whole tree had floated around in the sea, lost its branches, but kept its trunk intact.

Looking off to the right, I could see the river, barely making out the black blobs that were the rocks where I often walked. The crowd was much heavier by the pier because of the hotels bordering the beach.

"The pier is in the center of town, see?" Jimmy explained. "So there's a lot more stuff here."

Tourist stores sold flip-flops and suntan lotion and t-shirts with witty sayings on them. Stores with racks and racks of bikinis abounded. A little Dairy Queen sat on one corner, and a mini hot dog place was tucked in between a display of boogie boards and a shop.

"Come on," he said, tugging my hand. "We have to get some pier fries. The best fries in Ocean Park."

They were thick and brown, with plenty of salt, and came in a red and white paper box with grease soaking through the bottom. I drowned mine in ketchup. Jimmy poured some kind of oil on his. We stood at a right angle, shoulder to shoulder, breathing in the sun-washed air, the saltiness, and the sweet smell coming from the box in his hand.

We played the carnival games, really intellectual ones like throwing darts at balloons or using water guns to squirt at a target so the speedboat would rise. He won a little purple bear for me. It was plush and had incredible fake fur. A red ribbon encircled its neck.

Moving along the crowds of happy vacationers, I saw something strange. A girl strapped in a harness with two long elastic ropes stretching up to the tops of some poles bounced lightly on a balloon-like surface. She rose higher and higher with each bounce. Soon she was flying through the air, doing flips while she was high up. I pointed her out to Jimmy.

"I did that once." He looked pained by the memory.

He smiled again, and I felt like I was the one flying through the air. I would do flips for him if he asked me to. I would do anything for him.

## Chapter Eighteen

Early the next morning I rode Anna's three-speed bike to the post office. Crossing the main street, I passed early risers at their tennis games, racquets swinging. I skirted a group of beach-goers, bumping over the curb onto the sidewalk. The bike didn't have a kickstand, so I leaned it against the wall. The post office was the size of the kitchen at Whispering Pines, which didn't say much for it. Opposite the door was the window to talk to the man in charge of general delivery.

"Good morning." This morning a woman appeared at the window, probably a retiree who was bored with her new life. "What can I do for you?"

"The mail for the Burtons please."

She turned around, pulling all the mail out of the 'B' cubbyhole, flipping through the pile like a proficient secretary.

"Here we are," she said, "Burton."

A fairly thick stack of letters was handed to me. I put them in my backpack and rode home.

How amazing that I could think of Whispering Pines as home. I had hated the place, but now I couldn't imagine being anywhere else. Not even with Mother. I loved every nook and cranny, even the shower downstairs that had almost no water pressure. I even loved the third step that creaked and the screen door in the back that stuck when you tried to close it.

Riding up to it, I saw it in a different light. I loved the cedar shake shingles, the roof that seemed lopsided. I loved the pine trees that leaned their heads together and whispered secrets all day and night long.

Two of the letters were for me. One was from Aunt Joey; the other, from Mother. I opened the one from Aunt Joey first, ripping a hole in it with my thumb and sliding my finger along the top.

*Dear Kiddo,*

*I'm writing this in Tucson, Arizona. I've never been so hot in my life. The land looks like a stereotype, all desert with saguaro cactuses and many hills and canyons. Tomorrow I'm driving up to Sedona to see the Grand Canyon. As it is tourist season, I expect to come back much thinner from the press of the crowds.*

*Jane called me a few days ago. Something else, isn't she? She and John are the perfect siblings. I don't seem to fit into this family, do I? Just joking.*

*Give my love to Mimi and Ricky. I'll try to get back east and visit you before the summer is over.*

*Love, Aunt Joey, the one and only.*

The thought of Aunt Joey squeezed in with all those tourists made me laugh. She would come back with about three hundred new friendships.

Mother's letter was in a slightly yellowed envelope. The edges were dried and crinkled, like she'd gotten it wet and had laid it out to dry. My hand shook as I peeled it open. I hadn't seen her in almost two months, and this was the first I'd heard from her. The letter was written on a piece of lined paper ripped out of a notebook, the fringed edge still on. Mother's writing hadn't changed, still large and bold, sprawling across the paper.

*Darling Mary,*

*You know I love you more than anything. Taking you was wrong, and I know that. But I knew that woman wouldn't raise you right. I knew she would ruin you somehow. So I took you and raised you to be a strong, independent girl.*

*I hope you can find it in your heart to forgive me. I only wanted the best for you. Please come back to me. You can live in our old apartment, and Mrs. Lithby will keep an eye on you for me.*

*Love always and forever, Mother.*

I could hear her voice in my ears, filling them with laughter. She had two tones of voice, one filled with laughter and one filled with song. When she was mad she would start singing old songs at the top of her lungs. She yelled at me only once—when I broke her favorite lamp. I told her it was an accident, but in reality I broke it on purpose. I was so angry with her for making me go to school. It seemed stupid now, but I was in fourth grade then and what did I know?

She had known I was lying. I think that angered her even more than my breaking the lamp. She yelled at me, her voice hoarse with anger. That was the day I learned never to lie.

Mother had lied to me. She had brought me up on a lie, feeding it to me like candy. But she loved me, which was more than could be said for Anna.

My decision was never truly mine. I was going.

## Chapter Nineteen

The early Sunday morning was cool. I shut the window to keep out the chill. My backpack stood by the door, its canvas sides stuffed to overflowing with clothes. I wrapped a sweater around the picture Sylvia had bought me, and, along with the jars of sea glass, placed them in the bag.

My journal went in last. I felt like I was leaving something behind, a piece of myself in this house. I had truly come to love Ocean Park. I loved little Ricky in all his innocence. I loved Mimi for her naïve sense of superiority over everything in her life. She would figure it out in a few years and mature because of it.

I wouldn't miss John and Anna. John was never there anyway, even if I had wanted to love him. Anna hated me, but that wasn't why I didn't like her. She was weak and submissive, the definition of the walking dead, a puppet that responded when the right strings were pulled. She danced around on a stage for John, and when the lights went out, she flopped to the ground, unable to help herself even to stand.

I would miss Jimmy most of all. But I was young and still believed in things like everlasting love. We would communicate by letters and the phone until Mother was out of jail. Then he could come and see me. A few years and I would be old enough to get married. I wouldn't have to think about this pathetic, shattered family again.

The blank pages of my journal begged for some thought to commemorate this intersection in my life. I tried to compose a poem dedicated to this radical left hand turn I was about to make. But the words wouldn't come. They hid in the dark recesses of my mind, refusing to creep out into the light.

The journal flipped open when I lifted my hand. They turned to a well-worn page where the binding of the book was splitting. A deep ravine separated one chunk of pages from the other. My words, written in a crisp and even hand, conveyed my feelings of everlasting hope.

*Today is spring. Today is the new year, the new beginning. Not some cold day in January. The calendar doesn't matter in my world. I see the news on the ground, tucked away in dark corners, alongside someone's house, leaning against a picket fence.*

*Sweet yellow heralds,*
*Proclaiming news of renewal,*
*The joy of birth,*
*The new beginnings,*
*Cleanse yourself and everything else,*
*Go stand out in the melting misery,*
*And raise your arms in salute*
*To the sweet yellow heralds of spring.*

I remembered the daffodils that beat back winter's blanket of white. I remembered witnessing the new beginnings. Without a second thought, I shoved the journal in my bag and crept down the hall. I passed Ricky and Mimi's room. She would be glad to get hers back.

Out the front door into a crisp new day I marched. I was starting over, cleansing and renewing myself. I was pushing up out of the dank, cold ground, showing my face to the sun.

I was leaving home.

But I was going home.

## Chapter Twenty

Contrary to popular belief, hitchhiking is neither fun nor romantic. For all the Brad Pitt fans of *Thelma and Louise*, a reality check: Few cars will stop for you. Even fewer are driven by someone you would want to stand closer to than twenty feet.

I managed to get a ride all the way into New Hampshire from a sweet old lady who drove as though she were outrunning a tsunami. She weaved and ducked that little beat-up car through rows of vehicles like it was a video game. The crocheted cross that hung on a long string from the rear-view mirror swung back and forth like a pendulum, occasionally whacking the good lady in the face. Every time it did, she exclaimed, "Jesus, Mary, and Joseph, Heaven Almighty, forgive us for our sins!"

She cried that out without taking in a breath, making it one long run-on sentence. Then she drove right along as though nothing had happened.

She seemed to buy my story that I had family in Exeter. But her mind must have been going, for she didn't ask why not one single member of said family could spare two hours to come and get me.

She dropped me off at the Amtrak Station, nothing more than a wooden platform by a set of railroad tracks. Prospects for another ride did not look good in the drizzly weather. I jumped up on the platform to take advantage of the over-hang.

John sent up money every weekend he was too busy work-ing to come up. Part of it was earmarked for me. Except for an occasional ice cream, I'd saved it in a manila envelope. Counting the stack of bills revealed that I'd saved over four hundred dollars. I decided to take a cab. The nagging worries I had had before about spending his money were gone, re-placed by a devil-may-care attitude.

Then it hit me. I didn't know what prison Mother was in. I could go to Mrs. Lithby and ask, but I doubted Mother had written to her with a return address. She didn't even know I was coming.

My options were few. The first and least desirable was to sit on that platform, watching the trains go by until I died of starvation. Or I could take one of the trains back to Whisper-ing Pines. I could take a cab, ask Mrs. Lithby if she knew anything about Mother's location, and pray she wouldn't call the police. I felt so stupid now, thinking with my heart in-stead of my head. How could I possibly have thought this would work?

Another option that would solve nothing but satisfy my curiosity was to go to Manchester. I wanted to find out what John did every weekend that was so important. This was the most unintelligent and pointless option of them all. I took it.

The cab dropped me off at the house with the number I had read off the return address of one of his letters. It was a blue house with mulberry colored shutters, probably the own-er's nod to his wild side. The bright green lawn was perfectly trimmed. A straight path walked through it to the door, the driveway running parallel to it a few feet away. A square house for a square man whose life was a square box. Except for the dent in it, which was me.

Two cars sat in the driveway. The first I recognized as John's white Bentley. The other was a red convertible. As far as I knew, the Burtons did not own three cars. The jeep was still in Maine; the Bentley was here. I doubted that John and Anna Burton would own a red-hot chili pepper car. I imagined a leggy blond in stilettos stepping out of it, tossing her hair like in a shampoo commercial.

Instinct said to run away as fast as I could. My trouble warning was going off, sirens screaming and red lights blinking. Ignoring them all, I walked straight to the house.

All the blinds were drawn. I walked up to the high wooden fence and pushed at the gate. It didn't budge. But lo and behold, a pair of matched silver trash cans stood against the side of the house. Even the dents in them matched. Plunking down my bag at their base, I grabbed at the high window sill with my fingertips and hauled myself up.

This window's blinds were partly shut. Still, I could peer through the slats and see the whole room. Opposite me, a wooden bar was stocked with a selection of alcoholic beverages. The cabinet stood open, the padlock resting on the bar. I would have bet my sea glass that only John had the key. He couldn't have Anna indulging herself at home. Who cared what she did when he wasn't around?

Or what he did when she wasn't around. The T.V. ad model walked behind the bar. She flipped her hair like a shampoo ad and proceeded to make two drinks. Behind her came the recipient of the second one, none other than John himself. He must have said something witty because she laughed.

Maybe they were just business associates. Maybe they were discussing their patient cases. Maybe he was congratulating her on her new marriage or baby.

Or maybe they were having an affair. That seemed more likely since they began kissing passionately by the bar, the drinks still untouched. I almost gagged at the sight of their tongues.

My foot slipped on the garbage can cover. I looked down, realizing too late that it wasn't secured. I tried to adjust my footing, scrambling to remain quiet, but it would take a bomb alert to break those two up. Striving to avoid an air raid siren disaster, I succeeded in knocking the cover completely off, sending it and my body crashing to the ground.

Bomb alert! An entire percussion set played on the roof couldn't have made more noise. My leg, lying in the trash can, throbbed painfully.

"What the...?" A feminine voice.

Heavy footsteps followed. The door swung open. I tried to extricate myself from the trash can. Too late.

"Madonna! What are *you* doing here?"

*Spying on you, moron.* I didn't voice my thoughts. But anger flared up inside of me. Heat washed up through my face. This was my father, my role model. The one who was supposed to be faithfully married.

"My name is Mary. And what are *you* doing here with *her*? Did you get amnesia and forget that ring on your finger?"

I never saw him coming. He hauled me up by my neck, tearing my shirt collar as he slammed me against the side of the house. I could feel every bump, dent, and scratch in the siding.

"Who are you to talk to me like that, huh? I'm your father! No matter what you learned from that trash who abducted you, you've got to obey *me* now. You don't say anything about this, you hear? *Nothing.*"

His voice was tight and angry, but low like a snake's. A rattlesnake, that gave little warning it was about to strike, its subtle threat hard to hear. He stood right in my face with his clenched jaw. I believed that he could have killed me. I swallowed, my mouth like cotton, and nodded. No wonder Anna was so submissive. She liked all her body parts just the way they were.

He let go of me when his girlfriend called out.

"What is it, honey?"

He turned toward the front of the house. "Nothing serious. Just raccoons."

He bent close again. "Get your butt back to Whispering Pines, and keep your mouth shut." He straightened up and glared at me.

"Run!" he hissed.

I ran.

## Chapter Twenty-One

The rain hit the windows of the Amtrak train and splattered against them in a mass suicide.

*One night I flew*

The rain ran down the sides like the tears on my face that stained my cheeks red.

*In heavens so high,*

I was so scared, sitting all by myself in the passenger car. The conductor had checked my ticket a half hour before and hadn't returned.

*I saw the world's children,*

My chest felt tight, like John was standing on it. I could still feel his hands around my neck.

*Which made me cry.*

I put my hands up to my throat, feeling the torn collar. Feeling the tender flesh, which had no doubt already turned purple.

*There was blood and death,*

His voice still rang in my ears. Dark, angry, quiet, the kind that killed you. How could anyone survive for long under the assault of that voice?

*So much anger and despair,*

And the woman's voice, so carefree and happy. So unlike Anna's weary tones.

*Too many people hurting,*

Poor Anna. To have lived with that monster for more than fifteen years. To wake up every day and curse the one she was born on.

*And not enough who care.*

I wondered if Mother could have withstood the cold. I wondered whether she, too, would have melted and frozen over in submission.

*How is it that we live?*

Mother would have killed herself first. She was of the ancient breed of Romans who fell on their swords before letting their enemies claim them. She would have died to become free.

*Its ourselves we're killing,*

That's the New Hampshire motto. Live free or die. I didn't remember who said that. Some general on a rearing horse, forever trapped in a statue of stone.

*Pain, death, and hate*

The gentle rocking of the train that had seemed so painful now soothed and held me close. The tears stopped falling.

*Is all that we're giving.*

I watched the cold gray world fly by through the dirty window and the desperate rain.

*But hope is everlasting,*

The trees passing by were twisted and dark, but filled with a sense of purpose.

*It bears us on wings so white,*

Embodied with a strange beauty, they were living entities, each unique and thriving in its own way. They reminded me of the Ents from the *Lord of the Rings*. I loved Tolkien's works.

*Tomorrow is another day,*

I smiled in spite of myself. Everything would be fine. Things couldn't get any worse. I was still living, breathing. I was glad.

*Don't give it up without a fight.*

## Chapter Twenty-Two

Anna told me to stay in the house for a week. I was grounded—that was all.

I'd told her I had tried to run away, but that I'd changed my mind and come back. She accepted my story at face value. It was early in the morning and she was still reeling from the contents of last night's bottle.

John called, saying he was sorry, work was crazy, he just couldn't drive up. But he promised to come next weekend. Under her breath Mimi muttered her doubts. Anna didn't seem to notice Mimi's mumbling anymore.

I headed upstairs to my room, feeling the heat rise as I ascended. Mimi ran up behind me, grabbing my arm. Her nails dug in, creating little half moons in my flesh.

"I want to know what happened," she hissed. "I know you didn't just change your mind and come back."

"Ask your father."

My voice was neutral, but carried a threat. Pausing, she must have felt it. I yanked my arm out of her grip, running up the remaining stairs and slamming my bedroom door.

The room was the same, empty and lonely, the bed still neatly made. I pulled the jars of sea glass out first, setting them on the desk. Then I took out the picture, spilling clothes onto the floor. The nail was still in the wall at the same awkward angle I had hammered it.

I spent my whole day in that room, staring either at the ceiling or the picture. I dumped out all my sea glass on the bed, inspecting the pieces. I had over four hundred of them. The points were so high that I soon lost track without a calculator.

Ricky brought up a ham sandwich around noon time. Apparently, someone had gone food shopping. He knocked on the door with the cracked blue plate in his hand. The earnest look on his face would have made even John melt.

My eyes were closed by the time the cool evening breeze floated through my open window. The screen on it prevented most of the Maine killer mosquitoes from buzzing in.

I woke up to the sound of small rocks hitting the side of the house and twanging against the screen. All I could see was a dark shadow waving up at me. Only one person in Ocean Park was crazy enough to come to Whispering Pines in the middle of the night.

"Jimmy?" I called into the night.

"Shh. Come on down, I want to talk to you."

The back door stuck as usual. I pulled at it until it closed, then paused, straining my ears. I felt very Romeo and Juliet, very cloak and dagger.

His arms caught me up and pressed me close. Then we started walking, heading for the main road. In the darkness, my eyes adjusted just enough to make out the road in the moonlight.

"Where were you?" he asked.

I was glad he couldn't see the ring of bruises on my neck. I opened my mouth, then shut it. Should I tell him? John's wrath still hovered over me like an angry spirit. I loved Jimmy, and I trusted him. But secrets had a way of slipping out at the most inopportune moments. And he didn't really need to know.

"Oh, just took a ride on the Amtrak train," I said, trying to sound casual.

"Just took a ride, huh? Why didn't you come and see me when you got back?"

"Uh, it wasn't a parentally sanctioned field trip. Anna's grounded me for the week."

He laughed at that one, a short bark, then was silent. We got to the road and crossed it, walking down to the left before stopping. I knew where we were. It was a park, but not with the traditional swings and slides. It was a large group of pine trees with all the underbrush cleared away, leaving the ground a desolate brown with fallen needles all year round. Jimmy clicked on a flashlight.

"We're safe here."

He started in, the tree trunks forming a maze. He could only walk for a few yards before having to go around one. I followed him.

The light danced around the tree trunks. It would disappear, then reappear farther away. I kept walking into trees, scratching my skin on the bark, trying to follow that beam of light.

"Come on, come on," he said.

But the faster I went, the faster the beam of light seemed to disappear. I saw only sporadic flashes, fewer and farther in between, then nothing. I spun around, blindly searching, a dot appearing in front of my eyes. My shoulder connected with a tree, sparks of agony flashing through my body. I stood still, trying to control my breathing, to be silent enough to hear his. The sound of the crickets, and of the breeze running through the tree tops, blotted out any other sound. None of Jimmy, none of warm flesh and blood.

So when his hand clamped over my mouth, I screamed into it. He spun me around, laughing. My heart pounded; my breath shook.

"You scared me," I said. Talk about an understatement.

His only answer was laughter. He clicked the flashlight back on. The beam hit a nearby tree, forming a bulls-eye pattern. I stared at it, unaware of his lips descending to mine. Jimmy stopped.

"What's the matter?"

"Nothing, absolutely nothing."

I couldn't help thinking of John just then. Of his anger, burning cold underneath the surface, flaring up the moment he was confronted.

"I think I should be going back."

I started walking with purpose in the direction of the street. Jimmy stood still for a moment, and then ran to catch up, the flashlight's ray bobbing up and down before me.

"I'm sorry, I didn't mean to scare you."

"It's okay. I'm just tired. I'll see you around."

He walked me all the way back to Whispering Pines, clicking off the flashlight when we were close. The sleepers in the resting houses we passed hadn't a clue. I went up the back steps, yanking on the door. I didn't look back at Jimmy. I didn't want to.

## Chapter Twenty-Three

*And if I die,*
*My soul do take,*
*Carry me most high*
*In angels' wake,*
*Or cast me down*
*To blazing hell,*
*Do not worry,*
*But wish me well.*

John kept his word and came up that next weekend. Of course, everything was worse. Anna put on clean clothes and braided her hair. She smiled all the time, but her smile was tight and transparent, tissue paper thin.

The only one not affected was Ricky. He lived in the shadows, away from John's glare. He played by himself most of the time, content. When he was with other people, his endearing sweetness made everyone like him. He had grown up in a war zone, and like a blank child you see in *National Geographic* who seems not to notice the carnage, he did not see the pain and hate in this house.

I thought the most difficult part of the weekend would be Saturday. That was when we all went to the beach. We rode our bikes ahead of Anna. She strained under the weight of all the beach stuff because she had hardly ridden her bike all summer. I kept glancing behind me, watching her fade into the distance. John never offered to take the cart from her. We peddled down the streets under the shade of the trees until they thinned out and the sun shone down without impediment.

Ricky and I made a giant sandcastle at low tide, the wall rising a foot high around our tide pool. I uncovered a sandworm with my shovel. It was brown like its home and appeared to have little tentacles hanging off its body along the sides. When I dug it up, it wriggled, even after I had chopped it in half. I scooped it out and threw it across the wet sand.

It was an extraordinarily hot day, even for the beach. The land breeze brought only hot air and little pests from the dune grass. The pests got into my tuna fish sandwich, of which I ate every bite.

"Waste not, want not," said John. Those were the only words he said to me all day.

It hadn't been that bad a day, I considered in the shower, salt and sunscreen running down the drain. It was amazing how swimming in the ocean left me coated with salt. My skin felt sticky, but it was dry. When I piled on sunscreen over it, my skin became both oily and sticky. At the beach that was okay. Sticky, oily skin and crazy hair were part of the allure of a day at the shore.

Early Sunday morning, someone banged on my bedroom door. John opened it without waiting for my consent. I had a feeling of *déjà vu* as he stood looking at me, like the first night I had come to Whispering Pines. But this time I didn't stare back. I'd learned. Only a fool attacks a sleeping dragon.

"Get dressed. We're going to church in a half hour."

He slammed the door behind him. The first night I had wished he would slam it. Now I wished the opposite. *Be careful what you wish for*, I thought as I dressed. *You might get it.*

I found myself in a hard pew, copying the frequent standing, sitting, and kneeling of this crowd of Catholics. Mother didn't believe in God. The only time I remembered being in a church was for the funeral.

I expected an old man who terrorized small children to stand up and lecture us on our sins. It was an old man, but his round, merry face seemed out of place in the solemn setting. He began by wishing us a good morning. Then he didn't talk of sins, but of love. Loving self, family, and neighbors, even loving our enemies. I didn't understand how I could love my enemies. If I loved them, how could they be enemies?

My thoughts drifting, I glanced around the room at all the bowed heads. The few children present squirmed in their seats. Ricky flipped through a songbook, the pages filled only with words but still amusing him. Mimi stared off into space, apparently lost in her own little world. John sat in rapt attention, no doubt seeking some reassurance because of his double life. Anna did the same, probably because that was what John did. Her hands lay in her lap, twisting a piece of paper round and round.

Across the aisle a little old lady also studied the crowd. She was the first black woman I had seen in Maine. Her gorgeous skin was a rich, dark chocolate. She caught my eye and smiled. I looked away, embarrassed to be found staring at her.

After the service John talked with the clergyman, Anna at his side. I stood off to the edge of the stone steps, the hot sun beating down on my face. My feet itched in the shoes I hadn't worn all summer. The sundress stuck to my shoulder blades, adhering itself with my sweat. The lady from the pew walked right up to me, her steps strong. She swung her legs with purpose, beating out a rapid beat with her pumps. She walked just like Aunt Joey did.

"Ms. Fisher," she said.

She grabbed my hand and shook it. She had neither a southern accent nor one from the ghetto. Her voice sounded deep and cultured.

"Mary Burton."

She looked at me with surprise, big owl eyes behind her glasses.

"But aren't you John and Anna Burtons' daughter? The one who was kidnapped? Madonna?"

"Madonna is the name on my birth certificate. Mother calls me Mary."

"You mean *Anna* calls you that?"

I felt my face flush. "Not Anna. My *mother*."

Ms. Fisher stood still, looking at me. Her black pumps reflected the sun. I wondered if she shined them herself.

"Madonna is another way of saying Mary. You're named after the mother of Jesus, child. No matter which one you use, it means the same thing."

And she walked away, pumps clicking on the steps.

Madonna. Mary. In my mind they had been two separate entities. I was Mary. Madonna was a five-year-old kidnap victim. But Mary was Madonna, and Madonna was Mary.

I had just been too blind to see it.

## Chapter Twenty-Four

The sand felt warm beneath my feet, but the sky looked cold. Sylvia eyed the clouds, announcing that it would soon rain and I had better come with her. We walked to her home, up rickety wooden stairs from the sand, and onto the deck. Thunder rolled across the sky. I thought of angels with bowling balls.

We sat in her living room, before the twin bay windows, watching the storm. Lightning hurled itself down at the ocean. Zeus' anger spewed out over the whole region, heaving dark sheets of rain upon the sea, followed by the bolts of destruction.

Sylvia's lips moved as she looked out. They formed the same words over and over. I wasn't a lip reader, so I looked back out over the ocean.

It was only early August, not the time of year for thunderstorms, she told me. The really bad ones came later. Zeus calmed down, his might having been displayed to the mortals. The thunder rolled longer before rising and ending. I turned and asked Sylvia what she was saying.

"I was praying for all the fishermen still at sea."

I hadn't thought of the fishermen in their little boats, the great waves playing with them like toys. Like a young child in his bath, smacking at the water and his sailboat, indifferent to the havoc he wreaks.

The thought of being all alone out there in the storm loomed in front of me. If I had known how to pray, I would have just then. Sylvia took a shallow breath.

"My husband was a fisherman. Lobsters, actually. He didn't beat the storm."

Her hands were quivering, her eyes screwed up tight. But she didn't cry. Not this woman. Not the silver lady.

She didn't have to. I cried for her.

## Chapter Twenty-Five

Anna didn't lift her sticky hair off her neck anymore when it was hot out. Almost any female I'd seen with long hair would lift it up and fan at her neck. It had to be uncomfortable to leave it hanging down, sticking between the shoulder blades. But she didn't seem to care.

She actually got up one morning. Mimi and Ricky were watching cartoons. Neither one argued about which channel to watch. I was glad because there weren't that many channels to choose from in Ocean Park. But Anna wasn't watching the T.V. She was staring over her coffee cup at the wall. I wondered what picture formed in front of her eyes.

"When you ran away," she said in a slow, soft voice, "where did you go?"

She sounded disinterested, but I felt the question held great importance to her. I studied my bowl of Rice Krispies, watching them turn soggy and sink to the bottom. I didn't know what to tell her. I wished I could say the truth.

"I went to Portland."

She didn't move, nor did her expression change.

"Oh."

Home free, I relaxed, my muscles loosening. I stood up and rinsed my bowl out in the sink, the cereal running down the drain. I could see the back of her head in the window's reflection.

"You're lying," she said.

And then she got up, mechanically climbing the stairs. Not another word. Anna may have been empty inside, but she wasn't completely blind to the world around her.

The phone on the end table by the couch rang. Mimi picked it up.

"Hello?" She says.

She walked over and handed me the phone. "It's for you,"

The last time I held a phone, I was in the old apartment, talking to Mother. She was calling to say she would be home late from work, and could I please put the casserole in the oven? The next day she was arrested for kidnapping, and I was taken into custody.

"Hello," I say.

Sylvia's voice echoes in my ears.

"How would you like to go to the Clam Festival with me? You can take Mimi and Ricky too. I'm sure they're sick of the beach. It's in a little town not too far away. It'll be fun."

We didn't talk about the storm. She didn't mention my tears; I didn't mention her guilt. I hesitated for only a couple of seconds.

"Sure, I'll tell them to get ready."

Mimi complained until I asked if she would rather stay with Anna. Then she shut up and went to change. Mimi changed her clothes every time we went somewhere. The girl would probably dress herself for her own funeral.

Ricky asked what a clam festival was. I said I wasn't sure, but it was a beautiful day with the promise of fun.

Mimi and I sat in the back of the car. Ricky rode in the front with Sylvia. I could tell he liked her right away. They blabbered away at each other more than either one ever talked to me. Mimi had her nose buried in a teen magazine, reading some article too mature for a thirteen year old.

I stared out the window. I loved to watch the scenery fly by. Warm fields passed with crisp white houses floating among them. We went by a field with cows in it, a combination of black and white bow tie and plain Jane browns. An old man with a bald spot was walking his dog along the side of the road. With a start I realized it was the same old man I had seen from Aunt Joey's car. When we drove by he waved, and Ricky waved back with a nine-year-old's enthusiasm.

The sky was so blue it hurt—robin's egg blue mixed with shades of Caribbean waters. The sky alone made me shade my eyes to look up. The sun added its own brilliance, shooting through it with more hues.

The Clam Festival ended up being as much fun as I had indicated to my siblings at the outset. We got food from the many different booths set up in a semi-circle. There were clams galore, which I didn't like. The place smelled of French fries and fried chicken, lobster and greasy hotdogs. Sylvia paid for it all. I think she enjoyed going out with a bunch of kids. We ate under a yellow and white striped tent, watching a clown make balloons into dogs or swords.

There was a craft fair set up. Mimi bought a small plaque with her name engraved on it. She was so pleased she had found her name that she was friendly the rest of the day. I found a tent selling second-hand books. One by S. Birch was in an old carton. I bought it for fifty cents, a real bargain considering the popularity of the author. Sylvia laughed when she saw it.

On the way home, Ricky fell asleep, his head lolling against the headrest. The windows were all rolled down, and we sang along to songs from the golden oldies station.

Mimi was smiling, and I was smiling. Maybe loving your enemy wasn't too hard after all.

## Chapter Twenty-Six

The sun was in full force, kept in check by the occasional passing cloud. I took Ricky down to the beach so he could play in the hot high-tide sand with his animals. All we had brought with us were the animals and two towels. He didn't know it, but I was taking him to the ice cream parlor afterward to buy lunch. Ricky loved their French fries.

One of the small beach planes buzzed overhead. It was eggshell white and trailing a sign in the sky, "Marky's 2 Dinners for $19.99." Such sign planes passed a dozen times a day. I could hear them coming, and I always tried to read them. It was a marvelous marketing technique.

The sand stuck to my shins, oily from the lotion. I stared at the little flecks sparkling in the sun. Ricky was brown as a bear, but I could still burn, especially my face. I had gotten a bad sunburn earlier in the summer. My skin had peeled off my face in long strips, the flesh below a pallid white. It even burned at night when I was trying to sleep.

The seagulls hung around a lot more during the day because the trash output was greater. They flew overhead, screaming, "Feed me, feed me!" The pleasant hum of happy people filled my ears. English mixed in with the occasional elegant French. Little children played in the sand, happy lovers rubbed lotion on each other's backs, families made sandwiches and played games. One family set up a volleyball net near the dune grass. They were the worst volleyball players I'd seen. The poor grandfather kept having to chase the ball down the hill when his grandkids hit it too hard.

With one word I'd describe that day: contentment. To be content, to have joy burning in you, not passionate flames, but a slow, steady, dependable burn—this was to be treasured.

I flipped open my journal to a fresh page. My pencil hovered over it, waiting to embellish the paper.

*Genius*
*Is in the eye of the beholder*
*Friendship*
*In the palm of your hand*
*Love*
*Is over the mountain*
*Joy*
*Is upon the sand*

Sometimes I didn't know why I wrote what I did. It just came pouring out of me, and I had to put my emotions to paper. If I read it tomorrow, I'd be able to capture the exact feelings I had at the time I wrote it. That's what was so great about writing poetry. My poetry expressed me, and when I looked back on it, I was once again in the past. Good or bad, the poems always felt a little different the second time I experienced them.

"Come on, Ricky. Pick up your animals. We're going to the ice cream parlor. I'll buy lunch."

He grinned, shoving them into the nylon net bag. I shook out the towels, folding them up under my arm. One I used to dust off my shins. I carried my flip-flops down the wooden walkway. Ricky was already running along it, his heels kicking up. Food was a wonderful motivator for boys.

A thin concrete path crossed to the right between the dune grass and a yellow inn. We walked down between the parked cars and crossed the road outside of the crosswalk. I had Ricky get a table outside, but in the shade. He wanted a BLT; I got a cheeseburger.

Who should be at the counter but Jimmy. He smiled at me. I smiled back, but nothing got said. The smiles said enough. *I'm sorry, and I'm not sure what to do about it.* I placed the order and went outside.

Another boy who worked there brought out the food. He had braces and freckles and crazy red hair. He smiled, not at me but at my bathing suit. String bikinis with tropical flowers all over them tended to attract attention. I only wore it when Mimi wasn't around. She made me feel uncomfortable in it despite our silent truce. I still wasn't sure of myself around her, or where I stood. Jimmy was watching over the bar and through the screen door. I gave Red a flirtatious smile, making sure Jimmy could see. I marveled at the way we hurt the ones we love and how hate could turn into love and vice versa. I used to hate the beach; now I couldn't imagine life without it. Life seemed funny like that.

Ricky and I spent the rest of the afternoon at the beach. I felt bad when I got home because I knew Jimmy got out at five o'clock. I wanted to apologize for my behavior the other night. By four thirty I was showered and attempting to get dressed. I put on a skirt, then took it off again. I tried on a dozen shirts before I settled on a pink halter top and jean shorts. I looked older with my hair up in a bun. Jimmy always liked my hair up. He said he could see more of my pretty face.

By four forty-five I was walking up the side of the main street, hurrying because I was late. It took me almost twenty minutes to reach the ice cream parlor. I walked in, didn't see him, and cursed myself for taking so long. Red noticed my agitation.

"He just went to the beach, maybe five minutes ago."

I walked away without a thank you or goodbye. I knew what would happen. Jimmy would hear my apology and say it was all right. Then we would make out in the sand, like on countless other summer nights. The August air was stifling. I choked on it as I strode to the beach. Then I picked up my sandals and ran up the walkway.

Sand, sand, and more sand. But no Jimmy. I looked around, at first thinking to head toward the bustle of the pier, but then deciding to go right toward the seclusion of the river. I took off, doing the frantic business-man walk minus the briefcase...

...And stumbled right over him, hovering over a blond chick who looked closer to twenty than to his seventeen years. She screeched.

I felt nauseous.

"Wait, wait, I can explain," Jimmy insisted, scrambling to his feet.

Yeah, right. I had to get away before I puked.

If I'd learned anything at all from my parents, it was how not to put up with a man's lies, not to let a man walk all over me. John and Jimmy were cut from the same cloth. Both were charming and controlling. I had no doubt that to stay with Jimmy would be to give in, to wave my white flag, to lose my identity as a person. I didn't want to end up like Anna. Dead on the inside, dying on the outside. I heard Jimmy yelling, angry now. I kept walking.

Dry-eyed and head held high, I walked all the way back to Whispering Pines. Pieces of my heart lay scattered on the sidewalk behind me.

The stairs groaned under my furious feet. I walked right past my room into Anna's. She seldom got up during the day, preferring her alcohol-induced serenity. She was passed out on the bed, facing the open window. Drool escaped the corner of her mouth.

I marched over to the dresser, tripping over the empty bottles. They scattered under my feet like brown leaves in an autumn wind. I picked up her bottle of Vodka, took a swig, and tossed it to the floor. The liquid burned my throat, an angry dragon traveling to my belly. The putrid aftertaste almost gagged me. She had a bottle of Kahlua shaped like a little man sitting cross-legged. I drank from that, too, before smashing it to the floor. I could see Ricky playing in the yard with sticks in the dark soil, hidden away in a dark corner. He was oblivious to the world. Mimi was nowhere to be seen.

I didn't notice the sky beginning to darken or the labels of the bottles I drank from. I felt strange, like I was no longer in my body. My spirit looked down at this poor lump of blood and bone. It barely registered the screen door slam.

I could hear Mimi downstairs, talking to Ricky. All the bottles were smashed. I stumbled to the end of the hallway. The window over the porch had a broken screen, so it was never opened. I lifted it up with difficulty, crawling through the screen. The split in it wasn't large enough to admit my body, but I pushed through anyway. Blood ran in little rivulets down my arms. I didn't really care. I hurt more than any simple physical pain could. I wanted to bleed, wanted to hurt. Nothing was worse than the betrayal of love. Love, something I could never get enough of, always seemed to slip through my fingers.

The roof shingles were scratchy under my arm. When I moved, I could feel that some of them were sticky. I stared at the emerging stars, bright beacons in the sky, lighting up heaven—Las Vegas for the God I didn't acknowledge and all his good people.

Lights in the hallway clicked on. Mimi's head appeared at the window.

"What are you doing?"

I forced my voice to remain steady.

"I got drunk and I'm tired. I'm fine, really."

My voice slurred. She must have seen the blood, but she didn't say anything.

She had learned from Anna to keep her mouth shut and all the bad stuff would go away. But that didn't work in the reality where the rest of us lived.

Welcome reality.

Welcome winter.

## Chapter Twenty-Seven

*My heart is full of sunshine,*
*But my eyes are full of rain.*
*A sad parting so bittersweet,*
*From it none shall gain.*
*For goodbye is just 'til later,*
*Farewell a sweet goodbye.*
*But when you say those words to me,*
*I know it is a lie.*

Jimmy came over and tried to explain. Mimi let him in, staring at him with doe-eyes before leaving the room. She still hadn't forgiven me.

My head pounded and my knees shook. No matter how much I drank, my mouth remained dry. When the sun had awakened me, I was still lying on top of the porch. I managed to crawl back through the torn screen and into the bathroom before throwing up. The toilet had been cold against my clenched hands. If Mother were there, she would have held my hair and stroked my back. Hangovers were not fun.

I let Jimmy make excuses for a good ten minutes.

"You're slime, you know," I hissed. "I don't want to see you or hear from you ever again."

My speech may still have been a bit garbled, but his stunned expression told me he was getting my message.

"You led me on, using me to stroke your sorry male ego while you had Blondie—and who knows who else—waiting for you in the shadows. I...I hate you...and I want you to leave." I slurred the last few words, but they were still understandable.

"Are you drunk?" he asked in a shocked tone, clearly relieved to shift the focus onto me.

"I was. Last night. But it will never happen again over garbage like you. Now go."

Despite the calm in my voice, or perhaps because of it, he didn't move, but stared at me in disbelief. Mimi—I knew she had been eavesdropping the whole time—stepped back into the room.

"Hey," she said, "didn't you hear my sister? Get lost! Get out!"

Jimmy turned to look at her. The little girl who used to worship him had just done a one-eighty. Mimi had her hands on her hips, her jaw stuck out in defiance. I would have loved to see her take him on. My money was on her kicking his butt.

"Get out of this house!" she yelled. "Now!"

He blinked, looking like he had just been plugged into a socket and gotten the biggest jolt of his life. Then he dashed out, screen door banging in his wake.

Mimi mumbled to herself, then cast a pitying gaze in my direction. "I can't believe I ever liked him." She seemed to have forgotten that fifteen minutes ago she would have died for him. "What a jerk."

The words 'my sister' kept echoing in the part of my mind still functioning. I'd thought of her with those words for some time now. But I didn't have the guts to use them.

"I still hate you," she said.

I nodded. "I still hate you too."

She smiled a little and we hugged, holding tight to each other for a long time. Sisters were sisters, no matter what.

"I saw the broken bottles. If Mom asks, we'll say she broke them herself, and she must not remember." Mimi looked down at my bloody arms. "A shower might perk you up a little. You smell really bad."

That was the kind of thing one sister said to the other.

## Chapter Twenty-Eight

Puffy cumulus clouds spotted the sky. They reminded me of cotton balls. The blue of the heavens was more of an azure hue and didn't hurt my eyes. Rather, it gave me a deep-seated feeling of happiness.

I sat in a plush chair on Sylvia's deck. She was inside making lemonade. I'd told her the whole Jimmy story, and she said I did the right thing. Except for getting drunk and smashing all the bottles.

"Don't ever stay with someone who uses you," she'd said.

The S. Birch mystery I had gotten at the Clam Festival was even better than the last one I'd read. I was already half way through it. Sylvia set down two sweaty glasses on the table. I took a long swig of lemonade. It tasted even better than I expected.

"Thanks."

She nodded and asked what I was reading. I flashed her the cover. She laughed,

"Just what is so funny may I ask?"

"Nothing," she said.

"Nothing? You laughed at me when I got it, too."

She gave me an evaluating look. "I'm going to tell you something."

"Okay."

"My maiden name is Birch."

I sat still, waiting for the rest of her announcement. When she didn't continue, I wondered why she had said anything at all. Sylvia gave me an expectant look.

"And... Congratulations?" I said.

Maybe she was getting Alzheimer's; she was pretty old. When I expressed that thought, she laughed again. Maybe she was just crazy.

"Mary, I write under my maiden name."

And the light went on, the sun came up, and I felt really, really stupid. Sylvia Mathews. S. Birch. Sylvia Birch.

"You mean, you wrote all those mysteries?"

I couldn't keep my tone from sounding incredulous. She nodded, unable to conceal her mirth. I told her how much I loved her books. Then I asked why she never told me.

"I don't know," she says, shrugging her shoulders.

"Okay. I can deal with that."

The ebbing tide was more than halfway down. I suggested we walk. Because it had been cloudy earlier, few people journeyed to the beach. The waves were choppy and cruel. They probably had swept in a lot of treasures with their pounding.

I picked up a piece of green sea glass. The edge of a letter was elevated on it. There was a piece of brown by my feet, but it hadn't obtained the status of sea glass yet. Its sides were still sharp, and it retained its gloss and transparency. Sea glass is cloudy and soft. But it never breaks. You can throw it on the ground, stomp on it, and kick it at the wall. But it will not shatter. I tossed the brown piece back into the ocean. One day it would come back, after it evolved into its true beauty through trials and pains in the waves. What was left after its struggles would come back stronger than ever.

"Hey Sylvia," I called out.

She looked up from the ground.

"What?"

"I want to be as strong as sea glass."

Sylvia smiled at me, lips parting to reveal pearly whites. I didn't have to explain myself.

The next piece I found was indigo, so small I almost didn't see it. And then various browns, beautiful in their straightforwardness. Some partygoer had thrown his beer bottle into the ocean; all that was left was this piece the size of my thumbnail.

Sylvia called out. "Come here. I found something really cool. You don't see many of these anymore."

Something small and white was in her hand. It looked like a small wafer, too symmetrical to be a piece of sea glass. She seemed really pleased and proud of it, her smile as broad as the sky.

"It's a sand dollar. And it's not broken."

It was ivory white and perfectly round, a small tribute to the glory of nature. On the top were five oval boat shapes with pointed ends, arranged to form a five-pointed star. The bottom had a small hole in it that sand falls through.

"It's beautiful."

The ivory against her pink sweater made me think of strawberries and whipped cream. Without warning, I was overwhelmed with the beauty all around me.

I just had to look hard enough to find it.

## Chapter Twenty-Nine

Anna never asked about the broken bottles. She must have assumed they were a result of her drunken clumsiness. But she also didn't say anything about food—of which we were running out. She didn't eat much, just some crackers now and then. But there wasn't much left for the rest of us.

Mimi cornered me one day. "Dad's not coming up this weekend either. We need food."

I knew she was right. Our supply of peanut butter had dwindled to almost nothing, and the breadbox had been empty for a while. We were doing the best we could with what we had, but spaghetti got boring in a hurry. We had no fruits or vegetables. If we didn't do something soon, we would be subsisting on salt, pepper, and the contents of the spice rack.

"The store is too far away," I began. "It would take hours to get through all that traffic. And we need to carry a lot of food, so we can't bike there."

I looked out the window. The jeep was sitting in the driveway, a thick layer of dust on it from disuse. I looked at Mimi, then back at the jeep. She followed my gaze.

"Are you thinking what I'm thinking?" she asked.

I was. So what if I didn't have my driver's license. How hard could it be?

I told Ricky to stay in the yard till we got back. He was so engrossed in his game, he didn't ask where we were going.

Then we went up to Anna's room. Lying across the bed in a drunken stupor, she still hadn't swept up the glass. After checking the dresser and her purse, I began lifting up things. The keys had been hidden under a pile of the *Ladies Home Journal*. There were only two on the ring, one for the house, one for the jeep.

Driving was a lot harder than it looked, and I was even a worse driver than I thought. Mother had taken me out in her friend's convertible a couple of times, so I knew the basics. But I couldn't back up. And my corners terrified Mimi, along with everybody else on the road. The steering wheel grew sticky with sweat from my palms. Mimi looked like she was going to pass out, but she couldn't because she was the one who knew the way.

When we made it to the grocery store, I pulled through a parking space so I could drive out of the lot without backing up. We both sat there, remembering how to breathe.

"Wow," Mimi said.

"Yeah."

I had about two hundred twenty dollars of John's pity money left. We walked through the colorful aisles, pushing a cart across the tile floor. There were so many choices, and everything was so expensive! I would never have thought a box of cereal could cost so much.

We didn't have a list, but picked up anything off the shelves that we might need. We bought six gallons of milk because I was sick to death of drinking water. I worried we wouldn't have enough money.

Then we saw Lana. She bounded right up to Mimi, giving her a huge girl-hug.

"Hey! Where's your mom?"

"Uh, she's around here somewhere." Mimi's jitters showed all over. She'd probably never lied to Lana before.

Lana was too outgoing and bubbly to notice. Her dad came over and said they were leaving. I released the breath I didn't realize I'd been holding in. My lungs felt like they would explode.

We did have enough money when we included the five bucks in Mimi's pocket. The drive back was a little easier. Mimi knew exactly where she was going, and I took the corners like I knew what I was doing.

We had parked the jeep and finished unpacking the groceries when Anna came downstairs.

"Where did you go?" she asked, her voice almost inaudible.

We looked at each other. In unison we replied, "Nowhere."

## Chapter Thirty

The door to my room stood wide open. I paused at the top of the stairs. I never left it open. The basket of laundry I had been carrying was put down.

"Hello," I called out.

"It's just me," Mimi answered.

She was perched at the edge of my bed, looking at the picture on the wall.

"It's beautiful."

"It's me on the beach."

"I know," she said, awe in her voice.

The beauty of the ocean struck me every time I looked at it. In my mind the warm sun shone on my face, the sea spray scent surrounded me, the sand squished between my toes. The utter sense of peace I felt at the time had been captured with every stroke of the brush.

Mimi continued staring at it as she spoke. "Mom's going through a rough time. I'm sure she'll be fine. But I still worry."

"Yeah," I said, not looking at her.

The sunlight filtered through the pines and through my window, setting the sea glass afire like myriad tiny lights. The sand dollar took on an unearthly glow. The light danced across my bedspread, up Mimi's arm, and into her hair. The individual hairs seemed to catch fire. I studied the frayed edge of her jean shorts.

She looked down at the floor, then up at me. Her eyes glistened.

"I get so scared sometimes," she said. "So scared."

"Me too."

And then there was silence. A breeze came through the window, filling the room with the sweet scent of the pines. It battled against the stench of rising fear. At last good overcame evil, and the fear was chased out the door.

"I'd like to hear a poem," Mimi said. "I'm sorry about making fun of you before. I'd really like to hear one."

I thumbed through my journal. How does one pick a poem to read to one's sister, who is so scared and whom one used to hate? I kept going through the pages until I stabbed my finger down on one with my eyes closed.

> *Just as the tree bends*
> *But does not break*
> *So shall my spirit*
> *For it is made of steel*
> *And tied with love*
> *It forgives*
> *Yet never forgets*
> *My soul is strong*
> *It wards off evil*
> *But my soul*
> *Through love*
> *Will let you in*

She sat there in silence. Every time I read a poem to somebody, the emotions came running back to me, and I was back in the past as I spoke the words. But when the poem was finished, all I felt was his or her silence. Then the fear overtook me, and my chest tightened.

Mimi looked up, unsmiling." I kind of like it," she said.

She walked out the door, leaving it open behind her. I knew that was the best I would ever get.

And it was enough.

## Chapter Thirty-One

We found two twenty dollar bills on the counter in the kitchen. Anna must have seen the groceries and put them there.

I sent Ricky and Mimi to the store next to the ice cream parlor for some sunscreen and candy. The former we needed; the latter just tasted good. I couldn't go there for fear I would run into Jimmy. I didn't know what I would say to him.

Yesterday, Lana's mother brought over our mail, explaining that it was accumulating at the post office since no one had come for it in a while. The pile now rested on the kitchen counter. I started flipping through it. One letter bore my name. It was from Aunt Joey, dated two weeks before.

*Dear Kiddo,*

*I have a bad feeling. Sometimes I get a sixth sense about the people I love. "Intuition," some people call it. Personally, I think it comes from knowing and caring. But keep your eyes peeled for me, okay? I'll be there in about three weeks.*

*Love, Aunt Joey, the one and only*

She's crazy, I thought, refusing to panic. The remaining mail held no interest for me. So I picked them up, putting them in a desk drawer for John to look at later—if he ever came back. As I did, a piece of paper fell from the desk. It had tight, square writing on it. I started to put it with the other letters in the drawer, but the signature stopped me. Anna Burton. Why would Anna write a letter? I read it.

*Dear John,*

*I have found out about the blonde. I think I knew all along, but couldn't admit it to myself. I can't stand it anymore. I'm sorry I couldn't be a good mother, a good wife. I'm sorry I lost the baby. I'm sorry for Madonna and Miami and Richard. I'm so sorry. So I'm going to go away now, far away. And I'm never coming back.*

*Anna Burton*

Oh, God! Oh, God! Oh, God! No, no, no! Was I holding her suicide note? I dropped it like a burning coal. No sound came from upstairs. But none ever did. I didn't want to go up there for fear of what I might find. There had to be someone I could call, someone who would look for me. *But what if she hasn't done anything? What if she's just taking a nap or reading a magazine?*

I started up the stairs, clutching at the railing. Hot air pushed at me, making it hard to move. My mouth felt like the desert. Oh, God...I didn't even believe in God. I couldn't pray to him. The stairs seemed endless. I started counting them. There were seventeen total. Placing one foot in front of the other, I forced myself down the hallway to Anna's room. Slowly, I pushed open the door.

The curtains shifted in the slight breeze coming through the window. Her room looked just as I'd last seen it. I stepped inside. A strange smell hit my nose. Then I noticed the dark stain on the floor, stretching past the bed. I took another step and stopped.

She lay on the floor in a white dress, her neatly braided hair gliding down her shoulder. Her arms were crossed over her chest. Her eyes were closed, a slight smile on her face like she'd finally won something.

Blood was everywhere. The stains ran from her wrists over her arms and chest in a crimson tide. Puddling on both sides of her, it stained her dress and flowed past her bare feet to where I'd first seen it, just beyond the bed. Her motionless form rested atop a layer of broken glass.

*Close your eyes, click your ruby slippers together, and you will be home.* I loved the *Wizard of Oz*, and more than anything I wanted that famous line to be so. But when I opened them, I knew I was already home. And Anna—my real mother—was still on the floor.

I couldn't move or breathe. Something held me against my will, forcing me to gaze upon her lifeless body. I opened my mouth to scream, but like in so many dreams, no sound came out.

Outside a car honked, breaking the spell. I could move. I could run. Tripping over my own feet, I dashed from the room, slamming the door behind me. Then, with slow precision, I walked back down the stairs. I picked up the portable phone, stepped outside, and sat on the front steps. My fingers found the three correct keys. A voice resounded in my ear.

"Yes," I responded. "I need some help. Anna has just won. She's dead."

## Chapter Thirty-Two

The whole town came to the funeral. The old man from the jetty, Jimmy, Red. The balding man who walked his dog on the roads. The post office clerk. People I had seen on the pier, on the beach, in the ice cream parlor. People I had seen at Two Lights or the Clam Festival. The Barbie woman from the flea market. People I'd never seen before in my life. Sylvia held Ricky while he cried. Mimi and I held each other.

John finally showed up—without the blonde. He did nothing but drink, and his breath reeked like rotting fish and garbage. We stayed at Sylvia's house. I was glad.

I'd tried to contact Aunt Joey, but to no avail. She must have been on the road. Aunt Jane came up though, uninvited, at least by me. I saw her perm in one of the pews. She was with an old guy in an expensive-looking suit.

Relatives I didn't know I had came. Anna's sister Rebekah gave the eulogy. She had never told me she had a sister. Rebekah talked of growing up together in New Hampshire. Of long, happy summers spent in Maine. Of the pranks they used to play on each other. She began crying after the first sentence, choking out the words. Everybody cried. Rebekah went on to speak to us, Anna's children. Her loving family. Then she stopped, unable to go on.

We followed the coffin as it left its resting place, carried by the pall bearers to the waiting hearse. The doors opened, the light at the end of the tunnel. We walked to it, followed by the rest of the mourners.

People lined the walkway to the street. No cars except for the funeral procession traveled the road. Mimi stopped crying and stared out the window. Her empty gaze reminded me of Anna. I choked back my sob, but Ricky was still crying. I couldn't breathe in that car.

No one took the flowers from her grave. The great mass of people clustered around in all directions. It was on the bank of the Saco River in the beautiful cemetery I had once biked through. Dead silence in the presence of the dead. Not even the birds dared to talk. The priest said a few words and invited us all to pray.

"I would like… I would like to read something." My voice hurt. "I would like to read something," I whispered.

Everyone stared at me. I fumbled with the piece of paper, folded many times and soaked with tears.

I began.

*Such sweet sorrow,*

Sobbing broke out to my left.

*For pained were her days,*

The grandmother I had never met sank to the ground, Rebekah's arms around her in a protective embrace.

*The things I should have said,*
*In all the different ways.*

I stopped, my eyes burning, unsure if I should go on. Sylvia gave an encouraging half-smile.

*Tomorrow will I see her,*
*But tomorrow never came,*
*Bells sing their somber song,*
*A hurt I can't explain.*
*I wish that she were here again,*
*So we could talk and laugh,*
*I never knew her very well,*
*And now I never will.*

No one moved. No one said anything. I was used to the silence, but this one was broken by intermittent sobs.

Then Mimi looked up, her eyes dry.

"Exactly," she said.

## Chapter Thirty-Three

After the funeral, Sylvia brought us to Whispering Pines. No lunch was served in Anna's remembrance. Anna was a victim, but mostly of herself.

We sat at the table while Sylvia searched for something to cook. John had disappeared. A car door slammed. Nobody moved.

"Hello? Anybody home?"

Aunt Joey bounded in, kangaroo hop.

"Why all the long faces?"

I told her. Her radiant smile disappeared.

"I'm so sorry," she said.

Hugs all around, tight enough to hurt, felt so good. We had spaghetti. Aunt Joey and Sylvia didn't try to cheer us up. I was glad. Sylvia offered to take us back to her house, and Aunt Joey agreed. I pulled her aside.

"I would like to go see my Mother."

"All right," she said.

She drove me down into New Hampshire, to the women's prison in Concord. I don't remember a detail of the trip, except for the deathly quiet. The sky was blue, blue as the sea just after the storm.

We had to sign forms and ask special permission. But we finally got to a visiting room. The walls were so dirty.

Mother sat just across the glass. She smiled at the sight of me. I didn't smile back.

"I just wanted to tell you that Anna is dead, my real mother."

Mother didn't answer. I didn't expect her to. Her hair lay limp above her shoulders; her eyes reflected her change in circumstances. The beauty that had once shined so brightly before in my eyes no longer existed. Her faded prison tunic, frayed along the collar, said it all.

"You were good to me. You took care of me. But did you ever love me? I need to know—I need to know for sure.

"Baby," she said, speaking for the first time, "I do love you."

I couldn't say anything. I just sat there and concentrated on breathing. She didn't speak again.

"I'll write to you. I'll write."

She nodded and gave me a shadow of a smile. I left, knowing that it would be easier to pour out my heart on paper, that we would speak more truthfully through envelopes than in person.

Aunt Joey didn't seem surprised that I talked to her for only a minute. She followed me out. I noticed everything along the way, the dingy walls, gray floor. Guards in crisp uniforms. Bars. Automated voices telling me where to stand, where to walk. The bored face of the woman at the metal detector.

And outside, the sky. The sky that was now so blue it hurt. Or maybe that was what was left of my heart.

Jessica Biron

## Chapter Thirty-Four

The ocean crashed against the sand. A lone gull cried overhead.

I stood at the water's edges, the waves soaking the hem of my skirt. The salty spray reached up to me on the breeze.

Heat from the sun warmed my face. What I gazed out upon was the same scene that was in the painting hanging on my wall. The swells in the water rose and fell as far as my eye could see.

*Anna, why did you do it?* But that was a stupid question that even Anna herself could not have answered. She just knew it had to end. So she ended it.

A strong wave reached my knees. I thought of Jimmy, with his grin and his words; of John, struggling under his burdens. I wished I could forgive them. I wished I could forgive myself.

I found myself praying about Sylvia's husband and for the man alone with his dog who went fishing everyday, rain or shine. I offered thanks for Sylvia and Aunt Joey, for Mimi and little Ricky, for the time I'd spent here. Even for the trials and tribulations. By now the waves had done their worst, and I was as strong as a piece of sea glass.

The last page of my journal held a poem that would be forever engraved upon my heart.

*My love is like a phoenix,*
*Renewing everyday,*
*My soul is like a bird,*
*Longing to fly away,*
*My heart is like an angel's sigh,*
*Full of hope and pity,*
*My mind is like the eagle's flight,*
*Soaring above the city,*
*My hope is like the rising sun,*
*Filling me with warmth,*
*My body is like a temple.*
*Do not try to measure my worth.*

I picked up the jars of sea glass, flinging their contents into the sea. They glitter in the sun before disappearing beneath the waves.

They were gone, like my old life. I was ready to start again and collect new sea glass.

Aunt Joey and Sylvia waited by the wooden walkway.

"Hey," Sylvia said.

They wrapped their arms around my waist.

"Lets go dance crazy in the moonlight," Aunt Joey said.

Though no moon was out at that time of day, I knew what she meant. *Live each day like it's your last. Don't ever let it go.*

"Mary," Sylvia began.

"It's Madonna," I said.

She smiled at me. "That's a pretty name."

Hand in hand, we strolled down the walkway, three pieces of sea glass, ready to start a new life.

"I hope you'll like it here," Aunt Joey said.

"Yes, I'm sure I will."